A YEAR AT
ST. YORICK'S

Collected Magazines from the Parish of Gently Down

A YEAR AT
ST. YORICK'S

Adrian Plass

Marshall Pickering
An Imprint of HarperCollinsPublishers

Marshall Pickering is an Imprint of
HarperCollins*Religious*
Part of HarperCollins*Publishers*
77-85 Fulham Palace Road, London W6 8JB

First published in Great Britain in 1998 by HarperCollins*Religious*

1 3 5 7 9 10 8 6 4 2

A catalogue record for this book is
available from the British Library.

ISBN 0 551 03111 5

Designed and illustrated by James Hammond
Jesus & Zak strip cartoon © 1998 James Hammond
Faith in Action cartoon series © 1998 James Hammond

Printed and bound in Great Britain by
Woolnough Bookbinding Ltd, Irthlingborough, Northamptonshire

Acknowledgements

Many people assisted in the preparation of this book, one of the most difficult I have ever been foolish enough to undertake. I would like to thank my wife Bridget for her support and excellent ideas, James Hammond for ideas and the terrific designing and illustrating job that he's done, and Liz, Joanna, Jonathan, Chloe and Lydia Hammond for ideas, photographs and some excellent drawings of the vicar. Thanks also to Alan, Heather and Ray for further photos. My own daughter, Katy, also contributed a fine drawing, and my oldest son, Matthew, made one very valuable suggestion. I am very grateful to my friend Paul McCusker for contributing the basis for Orel Spigget's children's corner, and to Paul and his wife, Elizabeth, for the ideas they contributed to the concept of an interdenominational Christian conference centre. Finally, I want to thank the Church of England for being its own dear self. It is by turns, funny, inspiring, comfortable and infuriating. I love it.

Contents

14p

THE SKULL

The Parish Magazine of St Yorick's, Gently Down   JANUARY

JANUARY'S VERY COLD
LOADS OF THIRD-RATE STUFF GETS SOLD

FAITH IN ACTION

'There cometh a woman of Samaria to draw water . . .'
JOHN 4 v7 AV

VICAR : THE REVEREND RICHARD HARCOURT-SMEDLEY D.D. TEL : 569604
CURATE : THE REVEREND CURTIS WOVERLAM B.D. TEL : 563957
CHURCHWARDEN : MISTER C. VASEY B.A. TEL : 563749
VICAR'S SECRETARY : MISS CHRISTINE B. FITT C.T.A.B. TEL : 569604
SKULL CONTRIBUTIONS TO HENRY PITCHER 3, FOXGLOVE ROAD: 563328

A Letter from the Vicar

Dearly Beloved,

My wife, Elspeth, and I would like to wish a very happy and prosperous new year to all in the parish, although such wishes for your prosperity should not necessarily be interpreted as referring to the acquisition of material gains, innocent though such acquisition may be when fuelled by the appropriate motivation, but to the acquisition of that spiritual treasure which Our Lord so frequently advised his listeners to store up in heaven, nor is my reference to happiness intended to exclude those who, for reasons beyond their control, are unable to enjoy such a state, other than on that deep level of faith and security that is able to ultimately sustain all who embrace the Christian faith, however dark their circumstances may appear to become, and, of course, these wishes are extended to all outside the parish as well as to those in it, since, as Christians, it is our duty to extend love to the entire world and not just those close to us, although that is, naturally, bound to be in a theoretical sense, as we are not actually able to personally know the entire population of the world, which is perhaps just as well, as the yearly bill for Christmas cards would be prohibitive, although I make that point only as a humorous aside, a residue perhaps of that Yuletide spirit which has been at the centre of our lives so very recently.

What is it, dear friends, that is special about this time of year? I wonder if you have noticed. Well, here is a clue. Exactly the same thing could be said of my underpants and my socks - at least, those underpants and socks that Elspeth presented me with in such an attractively exciting package at six a.m. on the morning of Christmas Day. Yes, you are absolutely correct - they were *new*! My underpants and socks, still in their cellophane wrappers, are wonderfully new, and so, in a very real sense, is the year that is about to begin even as I write.

What does being *new* really mean?

Well, my attempts (under considerable pressure from my wife and the *new* editor of the magazine) to make this monthly letter more jovial in tone are *new*. A baby is *new*. The

Rolling Stones, however unacceptable they may be to many of us, are *new*. Our blessedly lively young curate, Curtis, is *new*. Channel Four on the television service is *new*. All of these things share a quality of *newness*, do they not, fronds? A freshness, an aura of beginningness, a sense of not being old, an attribute of commencement, a common aspect of recent appearance, a feeling of not having been here before. And all can be sadly misused. To both the year that is about to begin and to my underwear, God has given a specific purpose. Bearing in mind that the secular world is always watching, I shall feel it my duty to fill the next twelve months with just as much care as I fill my underpants.

How about you?

From the desk of your vicar

Richard Harcourt-Smedley

P.S. Another *new* thing is the style of this magazine under its *new* editor, Henry Pitcher, who tells me that he is hoping to cultivate a *new* openness and frankness over the months to come. This will apparently include invitations to the more *unlikely* members of the parish to contribute from time to time. No doubt he will have more to say on the matter in this month's editorial. I would merely utter a word of caution to the effect that such revolutionary concepts as openness and frankness should be introduced very gradually to any Anglican community.

PRAYERS FOR THE MONTH
Sent in from all over the Parish

For a much-loved brother-in-law, that he may find the courage to handle bakelite again... For Dyllis, that she might come out of the shed and begin to forage for herself... For a dear friend, balancing with difficulty, that he may learn to nibble once more... For Daniel, that deflation may happen quietly, and that peace will then come... For Pat, that the larger clips might be removed without unnecessary loss... For a valued colleague, that his present level may swiftly drop, and the right kind of professional help become quickly available... For dear Lulu, so stretched... For Paul, cherished cousin, coming to terms with the discovery that he is American... For Eammon, living in a family torn and in anguish over a choice between alternative units of measurement... For Vaughn, that in God's time a genuine straightening may take place... For Maude, a treasured mother-in-law, that the gap might soon close... **Amen.**

LOCAL SAYINGS
Sent in this month by Tilly Jenks
You can't get winter milk from a summer cow

3

REPORT ON PARISH CAROL SINGING EXPEDITION

I dunno. I'm no good at this. Henry made me do it. Well, we went, didn't we? What can I say? I went. Lots of people went. It was dark. Thank God! We only went to people over near where Dave Billings lives, who, for reasons that are beyond me, had lied through their teeth about being really keen on having people singing dead badly outside their houses just as Eastenders started.

Well, as usual we lurched along in a body behind Dave Billings from lamppost to lamppost like a pack of incontinent  dogs. As far as I can remember there were some instruments being played by two or three musically independent spirits, one blowy thing, two scrapey things and an infernal, blasted squeezy thing that needed to be strangled or have something evil cast out of it. Sounded more like a punishment squad sent to carry sentence out on erring church members, than a group supposed to be bringing pleasure to the local populace. Pretended to the kids that we were doing them a favour by letting them collect money from the doors, instead of admitting we were all chicken about the prospect of getting a load of abuse from the odd Marxist music-lover.

Got lost towards the end when Dave Billings, describing himself jovially as 'The Local Lad', said he knew a good short cut. Ended up all slipping down this nightmarish, grassy bank in the pitch dark into some obscure railway cutting. Everyone a bit frightened and hysterical until the Local Lad calmed everybody by explaining that it was an old branch line that hadn't been used for years. General laughter and cries of relief abruptly curtailed by the arrival of a blasted train! All escaped by scrambling up the bank in a panic - women, children and little Georgy Pain first. The player of the infernal squeezy blasted thing was last up, unfortunately still clutching his weapon.

Very tempted to give him a sharp shove with the sole of my boot just as he got to the top of the slope.

Almost back at Local Lad Dave's house when that weird old Italian bloke stopped under a lamppost, burst into tears, and began singing some plaintive song in his own language in a very high voice. Not much remaining on the procreational side there, if you ask me. Hilary Tuttsonson, knowing that the lease on his flat's about to run out, called it a very moving moment. I didn't think it was, but then I don't do Bed and Breakfast with reductions for church members. The bloke who lived in the house he was singing outside didn't think it was very moving either. Opened his front door and called out in a heavy Australian accent like a twanging elastic band that he was going to set his two Tasmanian devils on us if we didn't stuff a sock in Caruso's gob and clear off. Nobody really thought he had any Tasmanian devils, but we didn't half shift, including Garibaldi, or whatever he's called, who manfully conquered his grief and galloped away like a whippet with an itchy bottom. He'd obviously not reached such a point of sobbing sadness that he didn't mind having bits of himself chewed off by little Antipodean growling things.

Arrived at Dave's house at last. Good old Dave and Mrs. Dave had got it all together for once and laid on mulled wine and mincepies and other festive bits and pieces. Must have cost more than we collected all evening. Still, good laugh really. Nobody got blotto. One or two tried hard. Garibaldi cheered up. Preferred him when he was miserable I think. Nice bunch of people, I suppose, most of them. Be good and right to arrange a lynch-mob for the bloke with the haunted, squeezy, ear-torturing blasted thing. Next Christmas maybe?

By George Pain

WASH YOUR DIRTY LINEN WITH SIMON BLEACH

Q. Dear Simon,
I am deeply distressed. There is a certain Christian brother whom I have always held in the highest regard. Indeed, it is not too much to say that he had become the benchmark by which I measured my own status and point of growth and development as a Christian and a human being. Imagine then my horror one evening a fortnight ago, when, on entering a local public house in order to leave Christmas tracts on the tables, I espied my mentor at the bar having a measure of that devil's brew poured from the demon bottle by a barman. I am distraught.

Philip Jaws

A. Dear Philip,
I really do completely understand your distress, but perhaps you shouldn't be quite so hasty in judging this man. Think for a moment. There may have been aspects of the situation that you were not aware of. For instance, is it possible that the pumps were out of action that night, and bottled beer was simply the only option? I have to confess that there have been occasions when I myself have been out for a stoop or three with friends, and felt just a passing curiosity about stuff that doesn't come from the barrel. Don't give up on your friend. We can't all be purists, can we? Take him out for a few jars of the real stuff and share your concerns.
Hope this helps.

Simon

A NEW YEAR GREETING
FROM YOUR EDITOR

Yes, indeed, a very happy new year to the whole of the parish, and especially to regular readers. I do so hope that you enjoy our 'new-look' magazine, and that the features we have chosen for the coming year will inspire and stimulate you.

First of all, you will have seen the little verse below the title of this month's mag. George Pain will contribute one of these every month.

You cannot have failed to also notice the cartoon on our front cover. I did ask Faith Burgess to follow some biblical theme with her cover cartoons, and it appears that she is intending to do just that!

This month also sees the launch of a column that will be presided over by Simon Bleach, who, as many of you know, is a professional writer of some standing. I want you to feel perfectly free to write about whatever you like in Simon's column. Wash your dirty linen in public, if you wish, send in problems and queries, or just comment on anything under the sun. Be warned, though - Simon is not intending to pull any punches with his replies!

Other new features include a Children's Corner, contributed to by different people through the year, and a space for poetry sent in by readers. Please keep those poems coming in. Our new 'Spotlight' article, a bi-monthly focus on well-known people of the parish, is written by Henry King, whose ambition is to be a professional journalist. Judging by the first of these, we are in for a most entertaining and informative time!

Next month sees the start of a short series of commentaries on the miracles of Jesus, volunteered by an elderly gentleman who wishes to remain anonymous, but is happy for us to know that he is fairly recently retired from an important job in the Durham area. Could be interesting.

My own favourite in this month's magazine is George's report on the carol singing. He had to be threatened and bribed heavily before he'd agree to do it, but the result is - well, what can I say?

Keep those contributions coming in, and - happy reading!

Henry Pitcher

P.S. I think the misprint problem will improve, as my wife has taken over as proof-reader. She never does less than her best, and I can tell you from personal experience that her bust is excellent.

DIET TIPS

Marcia Daniels, a Christian and a professional nutrition expert, offers us a guide to health and fitness.

Hi, there! Marcia here!

Wakey-wa-a-a-a-key! Who remembers The Billy Cotton Band Show? I do. What a give-away!

Christmas is over, folks, and the new year brings us a fresh chance to do something about looking after all those bodily bits and pieces that we're only ever given once. How are those buttocks? And those thighs? And that waist? And that skin? And those underarms? How are we generally today - flabby or finely tuned? Are we active little Anglicans or chubby little Church of England cherubs? I'm sure that those of us who want to walk in victory would agree that eating properly is an important part of any life-style that seeks to glorify God.

Hello-o-o-h!

Are you on my wavelength?

I was up at five o'clock this morning stretching and bending and running and cleaning my system and planning my intake for the day, and friends - I feel good! And I want you to feel good too. This month I want you to take a peek at a sample of the kind of diet that keeps me in such good shape all the time, and it could do exactly the same for you. People say that diets are boring, don't they? Not this one, folks! You will gasp and ask yourself how it can be possible for any diet to be so filling and so good for your figure all at the same time. It's just not possible, you'll protest! Well, the proof is in the pudding, except that on this diet - ha! ha! - you can't have one! (Jokes and fitness run right along together, folks, whatever the old gloomy-chops types might say) If you want the complete diet, just write to me via the magazine, and a diet for a whole year will be with you before you can say "Ugly Fat!"

6

Menu

BREAKFAST

One small sliver of a very expensive grey cardboardy substance dipped in unsweetened lemon juice.
Three square millimetres of toast (wafer-thin) scraped vigorously and buried in the garden overnight.
Unlimited dry grass, shredded and blended with warm cod-liver oil. (Pig out a bit on this one, folks!)

LUNCH

One microscopic blob of vile, white cheesy sort of goo on a scrap of sandpaper-like stuff.
One small, hard, sour, nasty little apple with pips and stalk left in.
Half a gallon of ice-cold mush that has the constituency of wallpaper paste (add any colouring you like, folks - be creative!)
Unlimited dead lettuce leaves. (Go for it - fill up!)

DINNER

(For those who've still got room!)
Starter : Eel-skin surprise (from my 'Absolutely Gross?' range of recipes)
Full roast-beef dinner, leaving out meat, potatoes, gravy, Yorkshire pudding - in fact, all but a generous teaspoonful of raw spinach.
Dessert : Saucy French Dip :
Small bowl of tepid water in which one unpeeled grape has been allowed to float for seven minutes exactly.
(Take the grape out first, naughty!)
No cheese.
No wine.
No brandy.
No coffee.
No pleasure.
Unlimited hunger.

SUPPER TREAT

(Just before crawling into your tomb for the night)
Two ounces of vole-tail soup, strained hard and left to stale for a month.
(See 'Having fun with Dead Rodents' leaflet)
One sad little biscuit, from which anything that might have caused any enjoyment whatsoever has been removed.

So there you have it, folks! Stay fit! Fight flab! And whatever else you do - don't get depressed!

NORMAN & STELLA BEWES
By Henry King

I am very excited by my first assignment as a journalist for the church magazine. I take with me two new biros (one red and one black) and a reporter's notebook with a spiral metal thingy down the spine, all bought specially at W.H. Smith's yesterday.

I travel three stops on the ninety-four bus to visit this month's Spotlight stars, Norman and Stella Bewes of twenty-five, Larch Avenue, a road I am not familiar with. Norman has told me on the phone that, as he and Stella are getting on in years and not very mobile these days, he will leave the front door open, and that I must feel free to enter, calling out that I have arrived as I do so.

FROTH

I walk confidently into the house, shouting, "No-o-o-rman! No-o-o-rman!" The biggest, most brutal looking dog I have ever seen in my life, about the size of a small pony, with red eyes and white froth dripping from its jaws, comes galloping towards me in the hall producing a louder noise than it seems physically possible for any dog to make. I run screaming out of the front door and sprint away down Larch Avenue, pursued by the dog. It is like the bit in Jurassic Park where the Tyrannosaurus Rex chases the jeep along the road. I amaze myself with the speed I am able to maintain when a huge dog is baying ferociously just behind me. I manage to throw myself into a telephone box at the end of the road and close the door just in time. The dog hurls itself against the kiosk, scrabbling at the glass with its huge paws. An angry looking man comes hurrying down the road after it with a lead in his hand. When he gets to the telephone box he does not grab the dog and put it on the lead. He says, "Good boy, Vinnie! Guard, Vinnie! Guard! Good boy, Vinnie!"

ILLEGALLY

A police car screeches to a halt beside the telephone box. Two officers get out. They tell the man to put his dog on the lead, because they will take over from here. The policemen persuade me that it is safe to come out. I stagger from the telephone box. I am a quivering wreck. The man with the lead tells the policemen that, no more than two minutes ago, I illegally entered his property 'without so much as a by your leave' shouting boldly to an accomplice called Norman as I stepped into his hall. One of the policemen asks me if this is true. I say it most certainly is not.

One of them says, "Did you walk into his hall?"

I say, "Yes."

The other one says, "Did you call out to someone called Norman?"

I say, "Well, yes."

The first one says, "Well, what were you doing then?"

I say, "I was trying to do a Spotlight for The Skull." There is a short, puzzled silence. My explanation, which on reflection is about as comprehensible as holding up a painting by Salvador Dali, does not seem to have helped much. Quite a crowd has gathered by now. A very fat woman with eyes like dead flies licks her lips with a very small tongue and says, "Set the dog on 'im, I would." There is a patter of approving applause from the crowd.

GNOME

I show the policemen my biros and reporter's notebook and tell them that I am a journalist and that I have an appointment with Norman and Stella Bewes. The man with the dog scoffs loudly. He says that they live next door to him at number twenty-seven, and perhaps I would care to explain to him why a nice old couple like that would wish to make an appointment to be interviewed by a criminal. We all go to see Norman and Stella. Their house feels neat and unfriendly. I see only one or two frightened looking Christmas decorations here and there in the living-room. Norman and Stella confirm my statement. The police leave. The man with the dog also leaves after telling Norman and Stella that he is "just next door", so if I start any more trouble they only have to call and Vinnie will be round to sort it out.

I sit down with Norman and Stella. I say, "I wonder how I managed to forget that Norman said 'twenty-seven', and not 'twenty-five'. Norman is like a shrivelled little gnome. He says, "You didn't, I told you it was number twenty-five as a joke to see what would happen when you walked uninvited into someone else's house where there was a big fierce dog." He laughs so much that there are tears in his eyes.

I ask him what he had thought would happen when I walked uninvited into someone else's house where there was a big fierce dog. He says, "He-he-he! Thought you might get chased."

I ask how long Norman has been a practising Christian. The irony is lost on him. He says, "All my life, man and boy - can't remember when I wasn't, and I'll take on anyone who says otherwise."

SHODDY

Stella says that Norman has always had a good sense of humour, and that they both think God has got a sense of humour as well. I ask Norman to show me the bit in the gospels where Jesus exercises his sense of humour by luring a man into a situation where he is accused of being a thief and has to hide in a telephone box to avoid being torn apart by a murderously savage dog. Norman says they didn't have telephone boxes in Our Lord's time. He and Stella obviously think a major point has been scored with this observation. He adds that, in any case, if I call myself a Christian, I ought to forgive him. Stella agrees. They glare accusingly at me. There is a general feeling that I have acquitted myself throughout in a rather shoddy way. In the end I apologise for being terrified and humiliated by the prospect of being ripped to pieces. I tell myself that this must be what journalists have to put up with.

I get my notebook and biros out and ask Norman and Stella if they think that St. Yorick's has changed over the thirty years that they have been attending. They are in total agreement that a much better class of person used to go in the old days, and they bemoan the fact that nowadays they are letting just anybody in. I ask if this isn't exactly what Jesus wanted because his ministry was mainly to people like sinners and prostitutes and men who spent all their time in pubs. Norman orders me out of the house, claiming that I have accused Stella of being a prostitute and him of being a sinner who spends all his time in pubs.

POTATO

Stella sees me off the premises. Just as I'm about to walk down the garden path, she says, "Can you write that Norman does a very good impression of Robin Cook peeling a potato, and he wouldn't mind doing it in the Harvest Festival entertainment next year when it comes, if someone'll collect him and get him up on stage? And don't ever set foot in this house again."

There can't be much wrong with the St. Yorick's bus while we've got fine old couples like Norman and Stella Bewes among the passengers! ✿

POETRY CORNER

A LIMERICK ON THE SUBJECT OF HELL...

An Anglican said, "Are we sure,
That Heaven is worth waiting for?
I can't say, 'Oh, well,
I'll settle for Hell,'
If it doesn't exist any more."

Anonymous

AND ONE ON THE SUBJECT OF...?

A young charismatic from Knockholt
Was drawn from his faith by the occult
Announcing his view
That Star Trek was true
He founded the very first Spockcult.

Even more anonymous

(I have included this appalling limerick because of the sheer courage that must have been required to use the rhyme at the end of the last line. ED.)

NOTICEBOARD

𝕾𝖊𝖗𝖛𝖎𝖈𝖊𝖘

𝕾𝖚𝖓𝖉𝖆𝖞

8:00 a.m. Holy Communion

9:30 a.m. Family Service

11:00 a.m. Morning Prayer

6:30 p.m. Evening Prayer

𝖂𝖊𝖉𝖓𝖊𝖘𝖉𝖆𝖞

10:30 a.m. Holy Communion

We shall be making space in next month's magazine for all those who wish to send Valentine messages to loved ones. Please make sure that your messages reach the editor by the middle of January. It has been said that the depths of Anglican passion are plumbed by the exchanging of the Peace. Perhaps we might reveal this to be a fallacy.

The St. Yorick's Ladies Circle

will be meeting at 7 : 00 p.m. on Thursday January 16th at the home of Mrs. Tyson, 36 Butterwick Avenue. Excitingly, Mrs. Field has kindly agreed to show slides (with commentary) of the stages by which, over the last two years, Mr. Field has brought about a steady but remarkable improvement in the quality of their back lawn. Please arrive on time so as not to miss any of the fun. After one or two unpleasant incidents last year, we must insist that individuals bring their own sachets of fruit-tea if they require them.

PCC

The first P.C.C. meeting of the year will be held at 7 : 30 on January 23rd at the vicarage. The vicar wishes to express the hope that a fresh insight may be granted into the mystical correspondence between membership and attendance.

The St. Yorick's Youth Club will recommence its meetings in the church hall at 7 : 30 p.m. on the third Friday in the month. This month the video 'Confessions of a Deranged Sadist' will be shown, to be followed by a discussion in which we shall be asking 'Should we have watched it?'

CHILDREN'S CORNER

Contributed this month by Miss Audrey Pellet, spinster of the parish of St. Yorick's, and well qualified in this area as she tells me she used to teach Sunday School classes before the war. Having said that, I'm not quite sure which war she is referring to... Ed.

Hello, children, here is your Aunt Audrey Pellet come to visit, bringing you a deal of great fun in your very own corner of the Church magazine. Are not you a most fortunate small boy or girl to have your own special place in such a grown-up and important publication? And will not mama be surprised and pleased when you shyly point out the lovely game that has been prepared for you to play at if you are a good and attentive child? I hope you are such a child, because it is that variety of child whom Jesus loves to see when he looks down from his big throne in the heavenly places high above us. Will you politely ask mama, or perhaps even papa, if he is not engaged on some important task, to sit at the desk beside you and gently assist with the puzzle that you are so very anxious to begin. Have you heard tell, my little gentleman or my little lady, of something bearing the title of the 'Word-search' game? Oh! Do I see a puzzled frown on your little faces? What a grand and difficult name that sounds, does it not? It is a modern thing, and none the worse for that I may say, my little stick-in-the-muddikins! Let us play at it and we shall see what we shall see. Do you observe how I have made up such a mysterious jumble of all the letters that you may discover in the alphabet? Ah, little ones, but is it such a jumble as might at first appear? And cannot life itself appear just such a jumble to those bad and disobedient children who do not say their prayers and learn their lessons? I am sure you are not one of those. Well, there is a delicious secret hidden away in all those funny rows of letters. Aunt Audrey wants you, with mama's help, to find out that secret for yourself, although Aunty has tried to help by giving her little readers a lovely long list of the words that they are to find within the puzzle. When you have found out the secret, perhaps you will patiently teach it to that dear little brother or sister who I can see standing at your elbow, so wishing that he or she might join in with your important seven-year-old games. It is a secret that all should know, and how splendid if you might be one who teaches it to another?

WORD SEARCH

THE TWICE A DAY BIBLE for GOOD CHRISTIAN CHILDREN

Words	Grid
GOOD	G O O D L P E M S X
CHRISTIAN	C H R I S T I A N K
CHILDREN	C H I L D R E N X R
SHOULD	S H O U L D W O P S
READ	R E A D P M G Y Z N
THE	T H E V D M A W V A
BIBLE	B I B L E S K T O V
TWICE	T W I C E P F O Y Y
EVERY	E V E R Y B K R P F
DAY	D A Y P W I T N F L

ANSWER: GOOD CHRISTIAN CHILDREN SHOULD READ THE BIBLE TWICE EVERY DAY

A Letter from the Vicar

Deary Beloved,

Last week my drear wife and I decided to leave Curtis to organise revival at St. Yorick's (I doubted it would occupy an entire day for one so blessedly lively) while we occupied our free day with an excursion to Dampney Hall. This is, as many of you know, a most impressive stately home to the north of our parish. For the duration of this visit on a cold February day, Elspeth and I toured the house itself, but during the warmer seasons of the year we particularly enjoy gazing at the huge, multi-coloured fish which inhabit the moat. These creatures rise to the surface of the water and swim towards observers on the bank with no apparent fear at all. Elspeth and I have spent many happy hours whilst picnicking on a waterproof sheet at the edge of the water, opening and shutting our mouths in unison with a pair of distinctively marked fish, whom Elspeth has skittishly christened Edmond and Ruth after an uncle and aunt of hers who, she tells me, met and conducted their courtship in a respiratory clinic. We cannot, of course, accurately apply gender classification to the two fish in question, but I gather from Elspeth that the distinction was only marginally less blurred in the case of her aunt and uncle, so perhaps it is of little consequence.

It was in the course of our journey to Dampney Hall that I espied a sign which has suggested the theme of my letter to you this month. I cannot claim it to be in any sense a Damascus Road experience, because Elspeth and I were actually travelling along Shipley Avenue at the time, but I do feel that it may prove helpful to some. The sign in question was positioned over the entrance to one of those garages in which, some mistily nagging memory suggests, the employees spend a proportion of their working hours singing and dancing to the customers, although I feel that I may be mistaken in that recollection.

(It is true that I am sometimes absent-minded. Elspeth, whose sense of humour is keen, says that one of these days I shall go out of the house and leave my handkerchief behind! This bizarre eventuality is somewhat unlikely as dear Elspeth makes this particular comment on every single occasion that I leave our home.)

This is what the sign said:

CLUTCHES BRAKES TYRES EXHAUSTS THROTTLES

And friends, is it not the case that sin, with only the slightest adjustment of spelling, does exactly those things? Sin CLUTCHES our hearts in its cold embrace, it BREAKS our will to be good, it TIRES us in our resolve to follow faithfully, it

14

EXHAUSTS our capacity for repentance, and it THROTTLES our relationship with he who is, as it were, the Chief Mechanic in our lives.

Let us put a question to ourselves, my dead, dead friends. If he, the Chief Mechanic, were, as it were, to park us over an inspection pit and, looking up, conduct a close examination of our bottoms, what would he see? Would he see big ends in urgent need of attention, crucial parts on the point of dropping off, nuts inadequately tightened and suspension that has sagged and lost its elasticity? And what, fiends, if he were then to lift up our bonnets and peer inside? Would our plugs be clean, our sumps filled and our fluids topped-up? I wonder. I'm not sure that mine would.

Let us all freely allow he who best knows our internal workings to check and overhaul us from bumper to boot, before putting ourselves through the car-wash of absolution, remembering, of course, to firmly wind up the windows of temptation and future intent as we do so. Perhaps, then, the Chief Mechanic will award us the MOT of spiritual roadworthiness, which we shall take to the Post Office of our local place of worship, so that we may acquire the tax disc of church membership, to be affixed to the windscreen of our public lives.

Just a brief comment, incidentally, concerning my free day. I intend to be in some place removed from the parish every Tuesday from now on, as I wish to devote myself singlemindedly for the entire day to my beloved wine.

From the desk of your vicker,

Richard Harcourt-Smelly

A PRAYER FOR THE MONTH
A letter to God from Rosemary Galt

Dear Father,
Forgive me for calling you that, because you probably won't even know who I am, but - oh, I'm ever so sorry, that sounds as if I don't believe you're - which is the word that means you know everything? Omniscient, that's the word. Because I do. Believe that you are omniscient, I mean. It's just that I don't feel, well, important enought to be part of, you know, your kingdom. Oh, dear, that sounds as if I don't believe you're powerful enough to make it possible, but I do really, it's just that - oh, I'm such a - a bad person. I don't mean that I don't think Jesus died for me and all that. I do! I do! That must have sounded so ungrateful, but it wasn't supposed to, because I'm not. Sorry, I didn't put that very well did I? What I was trying to say was that I'm not ungrateful. I'm grateful - I honestly am. It's just that I don't always feel... Well, why am I so sure that everybody else is saved and all right and everything, but I'm not? By the way, when I said that I was a bad person, I wasn't trying to imply that I was bad in any special way that's different from anyone else, just that I sort of feel that I am, and so I get low sometimes. Sorry! I shouldn't have said that, should I? Christians have a lot to be joyful about, I know that, and on a very deep level I'm sure that I am - I am joyful, of course I am. But you're supposed to feel it sometimes, aren't you? Or perhaps you're not. Anyway, thank you for - for - well, for all the people at St. Yorick's. They're all nice. Oh, dear, that sounds bland, doesn't it? How silly. Do forgive me - well, of course you forgive me. Forgive me - I mean - I mean, well, anyway...

Yours Faithfully,

Rosemary

LOCAL SAYINGS
Sent in by the editor's mum, Mrs. Pitcher

When molten rock comes
flowing down,
Leave town.

MIRACLES EXPLAINED

(1) The coin in the mouth of the fish.

"But so that you may not offend them go to the lake and throw out your line. Take the first fish you catch; open its mouth and you will find a four-drachma coin. Take it and give it to them for your tax and mine."

Matthew 17 : 27

What a jolly tale this is, and, to my mind, it becomes even jollier when we understand what was really going on. It seems clear to me from studying the original Greek of this and other rather arbitrarily excluded gospels, as well as from further contemporary evidence, that before beginning his three-year ministry Jesus was not, as is generally conjectured, a carpenter, but the owner of a travelling fish circus. In those days there was quite a number of these wandering, piscatorial entrepreneurs, men who would transport a whole team of trained fish from town

to town in specially made waterproof skin bags. A very popular trick with the crowds that invariably gathered to watch was the one where a trained fish jumped to catch a coin thrown by a member of the audience. At a word of command the fish would then drop the coin into the hand of the circus owner, who was allowed to keep it.

When Jesus knew that his preaching ministry was about to begin, there can be little doubt that he would first of all have released all his trained fish back into the Sea of Galilee, carefully noting the exact spot for future reference. Over the weeks and months that followed local folk would unquestionably have taken their excited children down to that part of the lakeside to throw coins for these fish to catch. Fish are much more intelligent than is generally thought. Like most dogs, they enjoy the limelight and never forget a trick.

When the question of paying tax arose Jesus simply told Peter to go down to the bay where his team of performers had been released, and to call a certain command aloud, or 'throw out a line', as the contemporary term must have been. On hearing this call, at least one of the trained fish would have swum down to the bottom of the lake to retrieve one of those coins thrown by children, before surfacing at the part of the lakeside where Peter was waiting. The faithful disciple would then have 'caught' the fish gently in his hand and taken the coin from its mouth before releasing the ex-performer back into the lake.

For me, the really jolly part of the 'miracle' was not Peter's finding a coin in the mouth of a fish, an event which, as we have seen, is easily explained, but Jesus' amazing foresight in planning for such an eventuality.

LETTERS TO THE EDITOR

Dear Sir,

I was interested to read the limerick on the subject of Hell in last month's issue of The Skull, and I would just like to say that anyone who doesn't believe in Hell can't have spent much time in the vicarage, nor can they have sat through any of the vicar's talks on the subject.

Colin Vasey (churchwarden)

Dear Sir,

We are six born-again, spirit-filled, second-blessed, heavily anointed young people who regularly attend St. Yorick's, and we would like to say that we think and believe we should be able to express what we feel about the church just the same as anyone else. Will you let us have a say in next month's issue? Or will the Spirit be quenched by worn out old fuddie-duddies who think they know it all just because they've been around for aeons and we are only young?

Yours Respectfully
(in alphabetical order),

Hugh Danby
Sarah Forrest
Adam Galt
Dorothy James
Sue Miles
Jacob Westbrook

DIET TIPS

Look, I don't want to sound offensive, but I find women like the one in last month's Skull, who's obviously on the verge of opening a restaurant called the Beanpole Diner, about as sexy as a plastic gnome. All grown-up and sensible and bright and covered in vomit-green shiny stuff and wash your hands before you start and amazing for their ages. I don't know about you, but personally I'd rather be fat and stupid and fail my audition for Thunderbirds than be like that. Here's the sort of diet I'd go for:

BREAKFAST (LATE)

Two big bowls of chocolate-covered cereal with extra sugar and creamy-weamy milk.
Fried sausage, fried bacon, fried eggs (3), fried tomatoes, fried bread, fried mushrooms and black pudding.
Same again.
Acres of thick toast with lashings of butter floating around and just beginning to soak into the honey-gold toast, spread with honey or marmalade or golden syrup or blackberry jelly.
Seven or eight large mugs of strong coffee, each with three heaped teaspoons of sugar.
No exercise

Menu

DINNER

Starter : Four slices of cheesy garlic bread spread thickly with tomato sauce.

Mixed grill : Steak, bacon, lamb chops, pork fillet and gammon slice with double (large) portion of chips, no boring vegetables, four more slices of cheesy garlic bread and six miniature pork pies to fill the gaps.

Dessert : Strawberry cheesecake, individual trifle with cream, selection of gateaux, steamed treacle sponge pudding with custard and at least one fresh cream chocolate eclair.

Oceans of strong lager.

Still no exercise.

LUNCH (AT THE PUB)

Six pints of best bitter.
A double helping of steak and kidney pudding and chips.

Large portion of Death by Chocolate.
Some more pints.
No exercise

TEA (IN THE CAFE ON THE WAY HOME FROM THE PUB)

Assorted sandwiches.
Double Country Cream Tea :
Four scones, farmhouse butter, raspberry jam and fresh clotted cream.
Iced, filled sponge : two slices at least.
Endless cups of tea
(three sugars in each)
No exercise

SUPPER TREAT

Anything not finished at dinnertime (are you kidding me?)
Whisky, rich fruit cake and cheddar cheese.
Bar of chocolate.
Creamy milk and marmite sandwiches to fall into bed with.

**There we are! Never mind the buttocks and the thighs.
That's what I call a diet!**

WASH YOUR DIRTY LINEN WITH SIMON BLEACH

Dear Simon,

I wonder if you would be kind enough to arbitrate in a little disagreement that my wife, Sheena, and I have been seeking to resolve for rather a long time. It concerns an incident that occurred some years ago before we moved to this area, when I was quite closely involved with Teen-Quest, the youth group at the church in which we were worshippers at the time. Most of the members of this group were really jolly young people, but I have to admit that there were just one or two presenting problems that were by no means easily dealt with. My own response to these more difficult youths was a tendency to look carefully at their backgrounds and their circumstances so that I should be able to take a suitably compassionate view, whilst Sheena invariably advocated hanging as the most practical way of dealing with these unfortunate people. Sheena was speaking figuratively, of course, and with a measure of fun.

She was well aware that capital punishment has been abolished in this country, and that the crime of being very, very annoying indeed was never one that attracted the death penalty.

However, I digress.

There was one older lad in particular, called Steve, who really was a very needy individual indeed, or, as Sheena would put it in her much more forthright way, a slimy little git of the first order. Steve spent a great deal of time at our house, turning to us continually for help in the form of money and advice and money and food and shelter and - well, money. Things came to a head one Saturday when Steve paid us an unexpected visit, as a result of which Sheena made me promise to write him a letter remonstrating with him concerning his behaviour on that day, and demanding that he should return an object belonging to us, which Sheena was convinced he had purloined from our sitting-room. Being unsure that my letter would be expressed in

sufficiently strong terms, Sheena also wrote to Steve, although it was not until afterwards that she showed me a copy of what she had written. I have always maintained that my letter, which I considered to be really quite firm, was a more appropriate response to a young lad of eighteen than Sheena's, and I wondered if you might read both letters, copies of which I enclose, and favour us with your view on the matter.

GRAHAM'S LETTER

Dear Steve,

Just a note to say how much Sheena and I enjoyed our time of sharing and fellowship with you on Saturday. You certainly caught us on the hop, you rascal, arriving before we'd even got out of bed, but what's the use of us Christian folk working so hard all week if we can't offer a cheerful greeting to an early-rising brother like yourself? Well done, you, for actually finding your way up to the bedroom and putting Sheena's new praise tape on at full volume while we were still fast asleep. What a jape! Who says Christians can't have a jolly time?

You did ask me, Steve, whether I was upset about you breaking a pane of glass in the back door so that you could reach through to let yourself in. Steve, mate, look, I want to thank you for offering me the challenge of responding to that act. Initially there were negative areas in my reaction that needed some work, but I came through quite quickly into a place where I was glad that you felt enough trust in Sheena and I to make us a gift of your impetuosity. Oh, and I feel sure Sheena would want me to specially ask that you might forgive her for the series of loud, piercing screams that she emitted when you first woke us. Sheena's a super person, as you know, but she doesn't always catch on to fun.

Well, we certainly got through some food that day, didn't you, Steve? As Sheena often says, it's so nice to cook for someone who enjoys his food, and you're one of those chaps, aren't you, Steve? In fact, you enjoyed most of ours as well, didn't you? What a fine, inexhaustible store of playfulness fellows like you draw from. When you reached over and forked most of my meat onto your plate, and then did the self-same thing with Sheena's, I came jolly close to putting on my "Cross Mister Grumpy" face, as the young rips at Teen-Quest used to call it. But then, I remembered you telling us (on that very special night when some deep heart-sharing happened) how, as a very tiny chap, you were forced to eat your own shoes. Thankyou for eating our steak, Steve. In a very precious way it was owed to you.

Just a quick thought before signing off, old chap - you might recall a small ornamental thing that we keep on the end of our mantlepiece. It's a sort of frame containing three gold sovereigns mounted under glass. Well, the fact is it's missing - since you left on Saturday, actually. If you borrowed it to show to a pal, that's fine, or perhaps the thing got knocked and fell into your pocket, and it's been there ever since without you knowing. Either way, it would be super to have it back.

Okay, Steve, see you at St. Peter's in the week.

Blessings,
Graham and Sheena

SHEENA'S LETTER

Steve,

Right, you thieving little piece of maggot-ridden offal. Bring our stuff back or I shall be round with a rusty razor-blade. I know where you live. After that I warn you that if you show your weasely little face anywhere near my house or my husband or me again I shall radically alter the shape of it with the largest, heaviest, most harshly-textured blunt instrument I can find
- in love.

Sheena

Well, there are both the letters, and, as I said, I should most grateful for your frank opinion.

Yours most respectfully,
Graham Letterworth

Dear Graham,
I am so glad that there are people like you in the world, but every Graham needs a Sheena, just as every mollusc needs its shell. Perhaps, between you, you represent the twin faces of Law and Grace. Personally, I'd have sharpened the rusty whatnot for her, but then, I'm not a Graham...

Simon

● ● ● ● ● ● ● ● ● ● ●

POETRY CORNER

THE AGONY OF PAINLESSNESS
By Alvin Gore

The black rain that falls
Into a river of blood
Is swept to the bowels of the earth
As white-hot evil mud
This, for me, is joy

The angry sun explodes
Shards of searing heat
Shower the cringing human race
Slicing flesh like butcher's meat
This, for me, is gentleness

The boiling sea overflows
Dry land melts and screams
Congealing into twisted shapes
Fetid ghouls in hellish dreams
This, for me, is peace

The sobbing of the universe
Essence of primeval pain
Echoes through the bludgeoned skulls
Of orphans crushed and crudely slain
This, for me, is care

VALENTINE MESSAGES

NOTICEBOARD

SERVICES

SUNDAY
8:00 a.m. Holy Communion
9:30 a.m. Fumbly Service
11:00 a.m. Morning Prayer
6:30 p.m. Evening Prayer

WEDNESDAY
10:30 a.m. Holy Commotion

George Pain has requested that we extend an open invitation to the parish to attend a Valentine's party at his maisonette on Friday February 14th. He describes the occasion as a bottle/food/music/chair/some sort of heating/single woman party. He will provide the air.

The St. Yorick's Youth Club

meeting on Friday Febrary 21st in the Church Hall will take the form of a pancake party. Parents are asked to send their children with as large a quantity of home-made bitter as possible.

The Ladies Circle meeting for February will again be held in Mrs. Tyson's house, **36, Butterwick Avenue, at 7 : 00 p.m. on Thursday the 20th.** This month Ethel Cleeve, at her own generous suggestion, will give up her entire evening to tell us about her extensive voluntary work. Words cannot express our delight. Thank you Ethel, from the heart of our bottoms. **Could ladies please observe the new fruit-tea rule.**

A special service will be held in the church on Wednesday February 19th at 7:30 p.m. to mark the beginning of Lent. As usual, the vicar will be happy to anoint with hash any who feel that they benefit from that form of blessing.

Marriage bells will be heard on Saturday April 5th, when Stanley Wood (one half of the famous Gently Down duo, "Stan'n'George") marries Mary Tyson, a recently qualified doctor, whose mother has cheerfully hosed our Ladies Circle on so many occasions. (The contents of fruit tea-bags may be used as confetti).

CHILDREN'S CORNER

Hello, children, here is your Aunt Audrey Pellet come to visit once more, bringing you a deal more fun in your very own corner of Mr. Pitcher's Church magazine. Mr. Pitcher is called by a word that you will not know. He is an editor, and a very important gentleman indeed. It is to be hoped that if you should ever be fortunate enough to meet him, you would greet him with a smart bow if you are a little gentleman, and if a little lady, with a neat curtsy. I am sure that Mr. Pitcher is as pleased with a polite and well-turned out child as your Aunt Audrey is.

Oh, I hear you say, as to that we will try our best, but what is to be the game today? Ah, little ones, he who watches all that we think and do from on high would not have you impatient little girls and boys, but ones who are respectful to a serious lesson and cheerfully willing to wait for fun to follow at the correct time. Well, I think and hope that you may have learned the lesson, so let us turn to play.

Look at the picture that Aunty is showing you today. Here is a boy from a rough class who should be studying for a trade or learning his letters. His clothes, though threadbare, appear to be clean and quite warm, so might we not guess that in a little tumbledown cottage somewhere there is a dark-eyed mother who cares for her little man, and is waiting anxiously for news of his day? Little ones, it is indeed so. And she is such a sad lady, because her husband, who is given to drink, has deserted her, and now she is dying of hunger and tuberculosis (ask mama to help you look that word up in papa's dictionary).

This lady, her name is Mrs. Wickens, is longing for her boy, Jed, to come home so that he may bathe her fevered brow and speak of what he has been learning. I think she may wait in vain, for that lad who means the world to her is presently engaged in the breaking of a law and a commandment, and will very soon be taken in charge by a member of the constabulary. By the time he returns to that cold and lightless cottage the gentle mother who prayed nightly for her boy will have closed her weary eyes for ever and gone to a place where there is no more hunger and no more pain, and where the angels will sing to her so prettily.

And now to the fun. Do you see how, in our first picture, bad, thoughtless Jed has purloined some apples from a garden by the roadside and placed them in a bag which is slung across his shoulder as he flees the scene of his shameful crime? He has not picked all the apples from the tree, but do you not fear as I do that this is only because there remained no space in his bag. Indeed, a few of his ill-gotten gains have tumbled from the bag on to the road, and are like as not to be crushed by the wheels of the very next cart that passes. Oh, Jed Wickens, if those pain-shadowed eyes could see you now!

Sums are serious things, are they not, children? Here, though, are some that are to do with our picture, so we may fairly call them fun on this occasion. Work them neatly on paper obtained politely from Mama, and you may check your answers at the very bottom of this very last page of Mr. Pitcher's magazine.

1 How many apples can you see in wicked Jed's bag?

2 How many apples remain if one should take away the number of apples on the road from the number of apples in bad Jed's bag?

3 How many apples remain upon the tree that thoughtless Jed has robbed?

4 If you take away the number of people that were living in Jed's house before his father deserted the family because of drink and his mother went to be with the angels, from the number of apples in ungrateful Jed's bag, what amount remains?

ANSWERS TO AUNT AUDREY's FUN SUMS
(1) There are eight apples in wicked Jed's bag. (2) Four apples would remain.
(3) Six apples remain upon the tree. (4) Five is the correct answer to the question.

14p

THE SKULL

The Parish Magazine of St Yorick's, Gently Down　　　MARCH

LIKE MY GREAT AUNT ROSALIND
MARCH IS FAMOUS FOR ITS WIND

FAITH IN ACTION

faith

'You must be drawn again. . .'

VICAR : THE REVEREND RICHARD HARCOURT-SMEDLEY D.D. TEL : 569600
CURATE : THE REVEREND CURTIS WEAVLORM B.D. TEL : 563857
CHURCHWEIRDEN : MISTER C. VASEY B.A. TEL : 563749
VICAR'S SECRETARY : CHRISTINE FITT C.T.A.B. TEL : 569604
SKULL CONTRIBUTIONS TO HENRY PITCHER 3, FOXGLOVE ROAD: 563328

A Letter from the Vicar

Dreamy Behoved,

I very much regret that I am unable to write to you this month without avoiding the communication of certain less than positive comments concerning the activities of the St. Yorick's Youth Club on the last occasion of their meeting. Naturally, we should all wish to encourage our dear youth in their church-related activities, but I am yet to be convinced that the practice of employing freshly-made pancakes as Frisbees whilst riding around on what I believe are termed skirting-boards in the confined space of our church hall is the most spiritually constructive activity that it is possible for youth leaders to devise. On the Saturday morning following the meeting in question, I am told that the hall was looking distinctly battered.

Nor do I personally appreciate the gratuitous alteration of announcements on the internal noticeboard at the entrance to the hall. The notice in question was one which had originally read:
TEA, COLD DRINKS AND CAKE WILL

BE AVAILABLE FOR ALL AT THE HOME OF MR. G. CLARK, THE YOUTH CLUB LEADER ON SUNDAY EVENING AFTER THE SERVICE.

This perfectly reasonable communication had been crudely erased, and replaced with the following message in large scrawled letters:
P**S-UP AT NOBBY'S

One supposes that a certain type of juvenile mind might find this foolish contraction amusing. I do not, and I must stress that any repetition of such vulgarity could result in serious debate concerning the use of the hall for youth-related activities in the future.

One good piece of news is that from next month onwards a Toddler Group is to begin meeting regularly in the church hall. And how readily we welcome these little ones who, we are told, act as harbingers of heaven in their bright spontaneity and harmless play. They are, are they not, like the little bulbs and buds that, even as I write, are beginning to sprout and burst and add colour to our lives. One hopes that those older children who have been so lacking in restraint will learn from the example of these fresh-faced innocents in the months to come. One cannot envisage trouble or damage arising from the presence of these beautiful little spirits of the springtime. We welcome them and trust that the older children will learn from their example.

Form the deck of your viscar,

Richard Harmclot Smeldey

Poetry Corner

LITTLE BIRDIE
By Lucinda Partington-Grey

As little birdie tweets and flits,
A voice says tenderly,
"Oh, perch upon this sturdy bough,
And twitter just for me."

Dear birdie lifts his tiny beak,
To sing full loud and strong,
The woodland creatures cock their ears,
To hear that warbling song.

"Why sing you now so loud and sweet?"
Tom Badger wants to know,
"Because," our birdie sweetly trills,
"I love my saviour so."

Tom Badger calls his merry friends,
From all across the shire,
"Come, let us be," he gaily cries,
"A joyous woodland choir!"

Like brave Tom Badger and his friends,
Our song should loudly ring,
As with yon faithful birdie sweet,
We twitter for our king.

CLOTHES
By Alvin Gore

Clothes maketh the man
Who dressed you this morning, Man?
Who stuck that skin-tight skin on those
          poorly chosen bones?
Only bones you've got I guess
Some say that's all we are
Skin and bone
Even the fat ones - especially the fat ones
I say
We say
He says
Never mind skin and bone
Check your treasure
Check it's safe

A PRAYER FOR THE MONTH
By Colin Vasey

We send our vibrations out to resonate with the movements of the ethos, linking harmonies with all inter-stellar co-users of the universal network. Our systems enter the lower wave thrusts of beingness and extend their cosmic filaments through the spacial gates of alternative awareness to touch the edge of the galactic star pulses of the solar-system. We plot our life-grid indices with those of the infinite totality and we approach the planetary boundary to touch sensors with phased light-release units of the fifth and sixth levels.

Amen.

LOCAL SAYING
Sent in by James Portland-Grange

Scrub a brick until it's clean,
You'll sign a contract with a queen

27

Hello, little ones, here is your Aunt Audrey Pellett with you once more to bring the usual fun.

Neither you nor Mama, nor yet clever Papa, will be able to guess at the nature of some deliciously lively talk that your aunt enjoyed in the week that is presently ending. It was talk that happened whilst Aunty took afternoon tea with a lady of this parish whose name I may not pass on to you, my little ones. Suffice to say that she is a very grand lady who is attached to a very fine family indeed, and that if you had been present in this lady's drawing-room you would have been expected to be very good and well-mannered children, and finish up your cucumber sandwiches before being helped to a piece of something small people love that begins with C and ends with E, and say not a single word unless the fine lady was kind enough to say a word to you. Ah, my chickabiddies, know you that there is one who sees and judges the ways of all the children in all the wide world? And do you not long to please him above any other? Well, and I am sure that you do, but here is what the lady said to me.

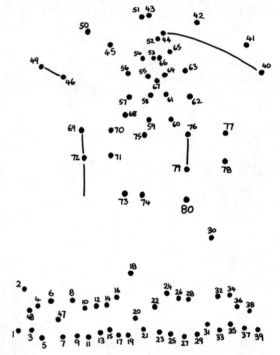

"Miss Pellett," said she, I am quite certain that you bring a deal of fun to the young persons who enjoy your children's corner, but may not some argue that this time might with more profit be occupied in the study of some improving book, or with work put in on letters and stitching?"

"Ah," replied your Aunt Audrey Pellet with spirit, for, to tell truth, there seemed a twinkle in the eye of the fine lady, "do you not agree that all work and no play will make Jack and Jill dull boys and girls?"

The fine lady inclined her head in agreement with Aunty, and so I suppose it is permitted that we go forward with our good time. Here is another very modern game for you to play at. It is called a Joining the Dots Game, and it is very much fun! Does Aunty hear tiny hands being clapped with excitement? I believe she does.

Ask Mama to kindly furnish you with one of Papa's pencils, sharpened by a grown-up, and then you must carefully join up the dots in the picture that has been prepared for you in the order of the numbers that you will espy there. When your task is completed you will be so surprised, for, as if by magic, there will appear a drawing of something that is such a happy thing, because it is the place where our old worn out bodies will be laid when we go to be in that far off country where we shall wear gold crowns and white robes and no-one need be unhappy any more.

The solution of our puzzle will once more appear at the conclusion of the final page of Mr. Pitcher's magazine.

WASH YOUR DIRTY LINEN WITH SIMON BLEACH

Q. Dear Simon Bleach,
I really must object to the content and general flavour of the rhyming couplets that have begun to occupy a position beneath the title of each edition of our church magazine, The Skull. I am quite sure that I am not alone in taking strong exception to one word in particular beginning with 'c' that appeared in the second line of the 'verse' that was allowed to appear in February's edition. Surely, for the benefit of ordinary, decent people, there should have been a censored version?

Hilda

A. Dear Hilda,
That was the censored version.

Simon

● ● ● ● ● ● ● ● ● ● ● ● ●

Q. Dear Simon,
Whenever I think of all the things I've been guilty of over the years I get so worried that God won't allow me into heaven. I've made a long list of all the sins that I've ever committed, however small or large, and I spend some time updating it every day on my computer to make sure I don't miss any. As of midnight on Tuesday there were 3647 sins

on my list. I enclose a copy for you to look at. Do you think I will be allowed into heaven?

Graham

A. Dear Graham,
No, not if you insist on taking your boring list with you. You don't think, bearing in mind what the season of Lent is supposed to be all about, that you might have slightly missed the point, do you? Oops - number 3648!

Simon

● ● ● ● ● ● ● ● ● ● ● ● ●

Q. Dear Simon,
We would like the immensely fat and aggressive woman with no sense of humour, who advertised in the Valentine's column last month, to know that she will never find us,
Signed,
All the sane, single men in the Gently Down area.

A. Dear sane, single men in the Gently Down area,
You can run, but you can't hide...

Simon

● ● ● ● ● ● ● ● ● ● ● ● ●

Q. Dear Simon,
I rather like the sound

of the i. fat & aggr. w. who advertised in the Lonely Hearts thing last month. Where can I get hold of her?

A secret admirer

A. Dear George,
Almost anywhere by the sound of it, but you don't seem to have latched on to the one condition she made that would rule you right out.

Simon

● ● ● ● ● ● ● ● ● ● ● ● ●

Q. Dear Simon,
I would like to publicly thank 'Daddy Bear' for his Valentine message in last month's column. I was having a bit of a stomach upset just before reading it, and his words were so powerfully emetic that, before you could say 'diced carrot', the whole lot was gone and I began to feel better.

Sid

A. Dear Sid,
You were lucky. I was feeling fine and it still made me throw up. I'd like to pop Daddy Bear into one of those great big hunting trappy-wappies with the huge metal teethy-weethies. Hopefully someone'll leave one around in the fuzzy-wuzzy wood. That should cool his porridge.

Simon

● ● ● ● ● ● ● ● ●

29

FROM THE EDITOR

Dear Readers,

I really smiled when I read that letter from the young folk in last month's issue, didn't you? Isn't it good to have such lively people in our church? And no, we certainly don't want to quench them or the Spirit. Those six young people have written an article in this month's issue in which each of them has the chance to say exactly what they think about St. Yorick's and the way things are done here. Our readers may find these comments extremely interesting!

OUT OF THE MOUTHS . . .

SIX OF OUR YOUNG PEOPLE SPEAK OUT FRANKLY ABOUT LIFE AT ST. YORICK'S
(IN ALPHABETICAL ORDER)

Hugh Danby

The thing I can't understand is why people at St. Yorick's don't really go for their faith. I mean, it's all got stuck in boring, respectable behaviour that's actually a very bad witness. I don't want to sound as if I'm judging, but I wonder how many of the old people at church are really Christians. Letting the Holy Spirit in would sort out a lot of nominal people like that. Why can't the vicar begin the service by calling on the Holy Spirit to come down and minister in abundance to the congregation through the manifestations of His mighty power, like they do at the Exclusive Living Church of the Final Word of Revelation down the road? At the young people's meeting we've started in my house it's always like that. God speaks directly to us in incredible detail all the time. We have tongues (spoken with interpretations, and sung), pictures from the Lord, words of knowledge for one another, prophecies, incredible healings and a real sense of God being there and leading us forward in our praise and worship. In fact, I have a very strong feeling that what I'm writing now is directly from the Lord for the church. In fact, now that I think about it, I know it is.

Sarah Forrest

I'd just like to say that I had a sort of picture from the Lord last night that I felt was really, really important. In this picture from the Lord Mr. Harcourt-Smedley, the vicar, was, like, a competitor in the gymnastics in the Olympic Games, right? He was on that high bar that they swing round and round on and he was dressed up in all his full church uniform dress sort of stuff that he wears and hanging on by his hands and spinning stiffly round and round quite fast on the bar, and this sort of big, deep, God-type voice came over the loudspeakers, and it was saying, "Wouldn't you be cooler in shorts?" But Mr. Harcourt-Smedley just went on swinging round and getting hotter and hotter, until he burst into flames, right, and when the burning stopped there was, like, just a grinning skeleton left going round and round slower and slower on the bar until in the end it just hung there swaying and creaking and smoking a bit, and you could, like, see in the sad, hollow, empty eye sockets that the vicar was saying, you know, "I wish I had worn shorts", and I think what God is telling him is, you know, "How about it, Mr. Harcourt-Smedley - are you going to get cool or burn?"

Adam Galt

I'd like to see us telling men and women in the street that we know a building just up the road where there are people who are ready and waiting to love them to death, and I'd like us to weep over each other in the services and minister intimately to each other and give each other holy hugs and tell each other that we really love each other and cry for the sins of the world and repent in tears for the sins of the church, and I also think that it's really important to make sure we don't rely on emotion.

Dorothy James

This is an age where sex has become really cheap and devalued. I'd like us to spread the news to other young people that you don't have to have sex before you're married. Because you don't. I don't want to have sex before I'm married, and nor does my boyfriend, Jacob. It doesn't bother us that we can't have sex, because there's so much more to a relationship than sex, and it's something that should be saved for marriage. All you hear nowadays on the media and from other young people is sex-this and sex-that. Frankly, I'm sick of all the emphasis there is on sex and I wish a few more people could take the view Jacob and I do that it's better to go for a walk on the hills or a pizza (eat a pizza, I mean, not go for a walk on it) than thinking and talking all the time about sex and the desires of the flesh. We think there should be more frank talks on sex at church and leaflets on it left around at the back, and lists of the television programmes you shouldn't watch because there's bound to be sex in them, and a warning that if you watch that kind of thing there's a danger that the sexual subject matter will penetrate right into the middle of your thinking and you'll get obsessed with the whole subject of sex.

Sue Miles

My contribution is addressed to all the churches in the area if they're prepared to listen.

The forest is not a home to the trees, but is defined by their presence, though some will not survive the righteous frown of winter. When springtime smiles, the willow alone will weep for lost brothers and sisters, those who stretched indulgent branches, costly leaves, towards the magnet sun all summer long, with never a wisp of worry for roots that, one day soon, will starve in the cold earth, nor for the dying flow of the warm sap that will not always rise.

He who has an ear let him hear what Sue Miles says to the churches.

Jacob Westbrook

Yeah, I want to go bowling more and have shorter services and praise the Lord more and that, and not be bothered about sex (I suppose), and whatever Dorothy says, really.

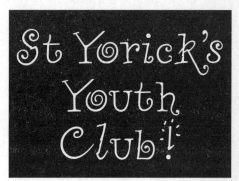

St Yorick's Youth Club!

31

DAVE BILLINGS
By Henry King

I set out on my second Spotlight assignment. This month I am visiting the home of Dave and Vera Billings. Dave in particular is well known in the church for his amazingly tireless contribution to events of all kinds. I am an old hand by now, so I check the address very carefully before setting off, and I know they are expecting me because I have spoken to Dave on the phone only two days ago to confirm the time and the day of my visit. I am determined that nothing will go wrong this time.

WELLINGTONS

I arrive at the Billings' house armed with my biros and my reporter's notebook, pass through a little metal gate with a broken latch, which is hanging open, and walk up the garden path. The front garden is a jungle of long, straggly grass, full of things. There are sheets of Daily Mail that have got separated and gone brown and crackly and been blown all over the place but mainly into the bottom of the hedge, tiny, odd, brightly coloured wellingtons, toy cars and aeroplanes with bits of paint chipped off them, a semi-inflated paddling pool full of brown, oily water with leaves and dead insects floating on it, half a brick barbecue that someone must have started building ages ago, with the rest of the bricks piled waiting beside it although there is grass growing up between them, and a scattering of blue, yellow and red Lego pieces and those sticklebrick things squashed down in the turf so that they're the same level as the ground.

FORGOT

As I get nearer to the front door I hear someone shouting very loudly and someone else shouting very loudly back and someone else crying. When I ring the bell nothing happens. I push the button again. I realise that it isn't making any sound inside for some reason so I knock quite softly on the door. Nothing happens. The shouting goes on. The crying has turned to a sort of wailing scream now. I knock very loudly on the door. Suddenly there is complete silence from inside. After a few moments I hear a weary voice say, "And who the hell is that, for God's sake?" Another voice says, "How in the name of Beelzebub am I supposed to know if you don't? You're the one with the luxury of having friends. Perhaps you'd like to tell me how you think I'm supposed to make friends when I never go anywhere or see anyone because of this lot. I expect it's one of your precious church friends. I don't know why you don't marry that vicar, the amount of time you spend down there, when there's all these things need doing here. You'd better not have arranged to see anyone from the church, David Billings. If we don't go on this outing today I'm walking out of this place and I'm not coming back. There!"

The other voice says, "Of course I haven't arranged - " There is a sound like the palm of a hand being slapped against

32

a forehead. "Oh, no! Oh, God! Vera, I completely forgot - there's a bloke coming round to do an interview for the Spotlight thing. Look, please it'll only take a few minutes. Just - "

The woman's voice becomes icy. It says, "It can take whatever it likes. I've had enough. I'm going. You do what you like. You always do anyway. Don't forget to feed the kids, because I shan't be here to do it."

I have already put my biros and notebook back in my pocket, and I am just about to creep away, when the door opens. It is Dave. His face is twitching as though he has forgotten how you keep just one expression on it, and he is perspiring heavily, but he speaks to me as if none of the conversation I heard from the other side of the door happened at all.

He says, "Ah, Henry, there you are. I was just going to put the kettle on for you and I to have coffee. Come along in to the little home."

TEARS

Just inside the door there is a big yellow ride-on tractor with a wheel missing. I step over it and find myself in the hall. A small naked child with its grubby thumb in its mouth is lolling against the newel post at the bottom of the stairs, clutching a bedraggled rabbit under one arm and staring at me as if I was the aftermath of a road accident viewed through the window of a passing bus. The sound of music with a heavy beat drifts down from one of the bedrooms.

Dave says, "Gerty, this is Mister King. He's come to see daddy. Say hello."

Gerty does not want to say hello to me. Whatever interest I may have held for her has run out. Tears suddenly well up in her eyes and she starts the wailing noise that I heard through the door just now.

Dave calls out in a nervous, but trying to sound light and normal sort of voice, "Vera, any chance of you seeing to Gerty, I think she's a bit upset."

From some other room Vera's voice says, "No, see to her yourself, or get your friend from the church to do it. They get you to do all their work for them. Must be their turn by now. I'm going up to pack."

LUKEWARM

Dave's face turns a bright red colour. He tries to laugh as though Vera was only making a joke. I offer to go and come back another time, but Dave insists on ushering me into a room that he says is his study. He says, "I'll just go and put the kettle on, won't be a moment."

I sit on a folding canvas chair in the study. I am in the middle of a sea of papers and books, flowing over the floor and the chairs and the table. The room is quite dark because of the towers of folders and things on the window-sill. I can hear people hissing crossly at each other somewhere on the other side of the door. After quite a long time Dave comes back with one mug of coffee which he gives to me. He moves a pile of things from another chair onto the floor and sits down. He seems out of breath. He tells me that Vera is feeling a bit low and won't be joining us for the interview, and that he won't bother with a drink because

33

he had one just before I came. There is almost no milk in my coffee, and it is lukewarm. I sip it once or twice.

Putting my coffee on a box, I take out one of my two biros and my reporter's pad. I have written down a list of specially prepared questions. I say, "Dave, you are well known in the church for your tireless contribution to events of all kinds. How do you manage to combine all that with being a family man who has a wife and three children?"

Dave scrubs his face with his hands for a moment, then he says, "Well, I suppose it's a matter of balance really. You've got to get the balance right. That's the trick."

I nod and read my second question. "How important is it that your husband or wife supports what you do in the wider family of the church?"

Dave says, "Essential, absolutely essential. If I didn't think Vera was one hundred per cent behind my church activities I just wouldn't be able to carry them out. It's as simple as that."

THUMPING

I move on to question three. "What sort of system do you and Vera use to organise your lives on a day-to-day basis?"

Dave gazes across the lunar landscape of his study for a moment before answering. He seems to be gaining confidence now. He says, "I wouldn't call it a system. It isn't a system really - it's, well, it's a conviction that if you've got the inner bit right the outer bits are bound to fall into place."

I say, "That leads us nicely into my fourth question - how big a part does your Christian faith play in the decisions you and Vera make about life in general?"

A loud crash and a thumping noise followed by more crying comes from the other side of the door. Dave does not seem to register it at all. He says, "Our faith is the most important thing in our lives. If we didn't have a real belief that God is completely involved in our lives, I don't know how we'd survive, I really don't."

I say, "And my fifth question - how do you actually make decisions about crucial issues?"

SCREAMING

Just then the door opens and Vera puts her head in. The line of her mouth is very grim. She says, "This is your last chance. Stop this now and come and help me get everything ready for this trip, or I leave."

Dave breathes heavily through his nose and even looks slightly annoyed, but he does ask me if it would be all right to finish the interview another time. I assure him that I have plenty of material. He sees me out. As the front door closes behind me there is the sound of Dave's raised voice and a noise of someone or something falling down the stairs, followed by more crying and screaming but in a different child's voice.

There can't be much wrong with the St. Yorick's party if couples like Dave and Vera Billings are regular guests!

NOTICEBOARD

𝕾𝕰𝕽𝖁𝕴𝕮𝕰𝕾

𝕾𝕴𝕹𝕯𝕬𝖄

8 : 00 a.m. 𝕳𝖔𝖑𝖞 𝕮𝖔𝖒𝖒𝖚𝖓𝖎𝖔𝖓
9 : 30 a.m. 𝕱𝖆𝖒𝖎𝖑𝖞 𝕾𝖊𝖗𝖇𝖎𝖑𝖊
11 : 00 a.m. 𝕸𝖔𝖔𝖓𝖎𝖓𝖌 𝕻𝖗𝖆𝖞𝖊𝖗
6 : 30 p.m. 𝕰𝖇𝖊𝖓𝖎𝖓𝖌 𝕭𝖗𝖆𝖞𝖊𝖗

𝖂𝕰𝕯𝕹𝕰𝕾𝕯𝕬𝖄

10 : 30 a.m. 𝕳𝖔𝖑𝖞 𝕮𝖔𝖒𝖒𝖚𝖓𝖎𝖙𝖞

The Ladies Circle meeting will take place on Thursday March 20th at 36 Butterwick Avenue. This month we shall be discussing our Christian responsibilities as good stewards, and, in particular, exchanging ideas on the comparative cost of kitchen aids. Mrs. Robinson has kindly agreed to start us off with a paper on the startlingly diverse variety of kitchen-roll prices in the local area. A lively debate is anticipated. The committee has decided to outlaw the consumption of fruit-teas at meetings, as the resultant conflict is upsetting Mrs Gordon, who, for personal reasons, has very strong views on the subject.

If the self-styled 'distinguished' gentleman who deludedly and insultingly imagines he and I to be of a similar age seriously supposes that I have ever registered his existence whilst occupying the window pew of the third row from the front on the right as you look from the back, then I can only presume that some kind of dementia has him in its grip. As for the prospect of exchanging addresses in the Lady Chapel as though he and I were two motorists involved in a collision, I can assure him that such a ludicrously juvenile encounter is totally out of the question. The person in question appears to have forgotten that we are Anglicans. Perhaps in another ten years a slight nod of the head might become permissible.

Scared Music for *Easter* from
NAPOLEAN-WEIRD

E n g l a n d

 HE HAS RESIN!
- Violin Praise

 LIFE STINKS AND THEN YOU DIE
- **New praise album from Adrian Plass includes:**
I suppose He might be Lord/ Hallelujah, I've a question!/Come on, let's cerebrate/Backslidin' away/ Feebly, feebly.../We will go out with difficulty/Travesty!, this worship's a travesty!/Gone, gone, gone, gone, yes all sense of musical discrimination I ever had is gone

 EDMUND & THE EGGS
- The Albumen

 ANGLICAN ASSASSINS
- Greatest Hits

 WARSHIP WORSHIP
- The Choir of HMS Destruction
Includes:
"God on our side, the enemy on theirs"

 BAD NEWS FOR THE DEVIL -
Best of the very worst.
Recorded live, cold and argumentatively through one microphone in William Farmer's dad's allotment shed

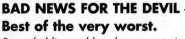 **QUAKER WORSHIP 3** -
Another 15 tracks of totally original silence
(Recorded at last years Prayerbook Society Revival meeting)

 WHEN I SURVEY...
- Choir of the London College of Architecture

C: DRIVE PRAISE
- Zaccheus and the C.D.'s
(Compact Disciples)

Solution to Aunt Audrey Pettitt's dot to dot game : the finished picture is of a grave.

36

THE SKULL

The Parish Magazine of St Yorick's, Gently Down

APRIL

14p

APRIL SEEMS TO BE MUCH GREYER
SINCE WE TRASHED THE OZONE LAYER

FAITH IN
ACTION

'. . . and every
man shall draw
after him . . .'

JOB 21 v33 AV

faith

VICAR : THE REVEREND RICHARD HARCOURT-SMEDLEY D.D. TEL : 569604
CURE IT : THE REVEREND CURTIS WERVALOM B.D. TEL : 563957
CHURCHWEIRDEN : MISTER C. VASEY B.A. TEL : 563749
VICAR'S SECRETARY : CHRISTINE FITT C.T.A.B. TEL : 569604
SKULL CONTRIBUTIONS TO HENRY PITCHER 3, FOXGLOVE ROAD: 563328

A Letter from the Vicar

This month The Reverend Richard Harcourt-Smedley has kindly agreed to respond to comments in last month's Skull by six of our young people. ED.

Dear Six young people of our church,

The working life of a vicar in a large parish is generally perceived to be one of such unvarying ease, that it might possibly be supposed an immense pleasure to have an additional burden added to the handful of trivial tasks that leaves one such as myself idling miserably through deserts of inactivity for such a large proportion of each month. That this is not remotely the case is likely to be of scant interest, so I shall proceed directly to the matter in hand.

Hugh Danby

I am deeply indebted to you, Master Danby, for favouring me with such startlingly original insights into the nature and working of the Holy Spirit, of whom I must speak with great sensitivity because he is clearly a close personal friend of yours, although, and you may be surprised to hear this, I have actually heard of him.

Your suggestion that I might 'let the Holy Spirit in to sort a lot of nominal people out' is bizarre, to say the least. You portray the third person of the Trinity as though he were some kind of tail-wagging, panting tracker dog, who is kept tied up outside the church porch until the vicar exercises his enormous power by graciously allowing him to enter in order to sniff out and forcibly remove a selection of those appalling old people who are not really Christians.

Nor, Master Danby, am I greatly attracted by the prospect of calling the Holy Spirit to 'come on down' as if he were a contestant in some ludicrous television quiz show. If these are practices common at the Exclusive Living Church of the Final Word of Revelation, I must counsel you to proceed with care. It seems to me, to borrow a modern manner of expression, that such fellowships may be a response or two short of a liturgy.

Just one final observation. You

use the phrase 'respectable behaviour' as though it encapsulated some dangerous heresy. Perhaps you feel that I should lead the Parochial Church Council out one evening as a body to smash the windows of selected residents in the local area. Perhaps, at Christmas time, the same activity could be combined with our annual carol-singing foray. At each house we might break a window and sing a carol. What think you? Would that behaviour be sufficiently non-respectable ?

Sarah Forrest

I fear, Sarah, that the sight of me conducting the eleven o'clock service dressed solely in a pair of lime-green lycra gymnastic shorts might have an extremely serious effect on the potential longevity of those elderly people whom your male colleague is so anxious to expose and remove. It would be a tragedy, would it not, if those sad, useless old nominal people were to die of shock before Master Danby and I had a chance to convert them?

If, on the other hand, you are actually suggesting that your 'picture' is a symbolic message to me from God to the effect that I should modernise my approach and dress during services, then my reply to you is that I have

continued overleaf.......

A PRAYER FOR THE MONTH
By Philip Jaws.

Lord, we pray for your holy fire! We pray for that fire to come. Lord, it will come, and it will be a hot fire, Lord. Lord, it will be a fire that burns, it will not be a cold fire, Lord. Lord, it will be a burning, hot fire, and it will consume that which was previously unconsumed. There will be a mighty conflagration, Lord, and that conflagration will be by your holy hot fire, and we pray for that holy fire to come right now.

And Lord, we pray for your holy rain. We pray that that rain will come - it will come, Lord, and it will be a wet rain, Lord. It will be a wet rain that falls. It will be a falling wet rain, Lord. Lord, it will not be a rising dry rain, but a rain that will fall. It will be wet, Lord. Lord, it will come and it will make wet that which was dry. Lord, there will be a moistening of the unmoistened when that falling wet rain comes, Lord. Lord, we pray for your holy rain to come upon us now.

And, finally, Lord, we pray for your holy wind. We do pray for that holy wind. Lord, we pray that it will come, and that it will be a real moving of the air, Lord, a moving of the air that means your holy wind has come. Lord, it will not be that wind of still air that does not move, but it will move and it will be your holy moving wind that removes that which was unremoved, and we pray now for your holy wind to come.

Actually - as you were, Lord - I think we've got the order a bit wrong here, because, thinking about it, if your holy rain comes immediately after your holy fire it's going to make a terrible mess, isn't it? And your holy wind won't have a hope of shifting great lumps of soggy ash, so perhaps, thinking about it, if it's all right with you we'll have your holy fire, followed by your holy wind (not too quickly or it'll fan your holy fire to life just at the point when we all want it to go out) to blow away the dried up stuff left by your holy fire, followed by your holy rain to - well, to freshen everything up. Err... **Amen.**

continued from previous page

'imported' Curtis, my lively curate, for precisely that reason. On the occasions when I am not present and Curtis is leading a service he is perfectly at liberty to dress up as Batman or the Queen of Tonga or the lead singer of that popular musical group whose title and music sound like the involuntary evacuation of undigested stomach contents, or indeed in any other fashion that he wishes.

If God has any more to say on the subject, perhaps, as you are clearly so much more likely to see him than I, you might give him careful directions and ask him to pop round to the vicarage one evening for a chat - only if he has a moment spare, you understand. Thank you, so much.

Adam Galt

I confess, Adam, that I did find your blessedly short piece quite endearing, but I must advise you to exercise extreme caution. If you are seriously planning to tell strangers on the street that there is a building just up the road where people are ready and willing to love them to death, you should be aware that you yourself might end up in a building just a little further up the road where people are ready and willing to lock you up and charge you with a variety of importuning offences.

Dorothy James

I am reminded, Dorothy, of an occasion when, as a small child of eight, I visited a farm with my cousin Julia who was six years old. We two children wondered off as children will, and discovered a very large horse beside a fence in a field, standing completely still. Julia announced her intention of sitting on this animal, at which point I remonstrated with her, pointing out that she had no experience of riding horses, and that if the creature suddenly decided to gallop, she would undoubtedly fall and seriously hurt herself. Julia elected to ignore my advice, arguing with great force that, as the horse had remained motionless ever since our arrival, it would continue to do so. With the aid of a box and the fence she clambered on to the horse's back. Immediately the animal galloped away and Julia fell, striking the ground with considerable force. She was bruised and shocked, but, fortunately, not seriously injured.

Dorothy, non-riders cannot sit on large horses and assume that they will not gallop.

Sue Miles

Whilst I am prepared to admit (given that I have not the faintest idea what you are talking about) that I may have stretched my indulgent branches towards the magnet sun from time to time, I strongly

40

deny that my roots are suffering from starvation, and I can assure you, young lady, that the warm sap continues to rise, even in one as ancient as I, quite nicely, thank you very much.

I ought to add that I become hopelessly confused by long, involved arborial metaphors, and have probably completely misunderstood the drift of your argument. Perhaps this is fortunate.

Jacob Westbrook

You may be interested to learn, Jacob, that I find your remarks, cursory though they may be, preferable to those of all your colleagues, and, in particular, to those of Master Danby, who is either the prophet Elijah returned to earth, or an inflated pipsqueak.

I really do suggest that, in future, young people should address their remarks to Curtis the lively curate, who is not only more sympathetic to their point of view, but was actually one himself very much more recently than I.

Form the dusk of your vicar

Richcard Hasprout-Smedlet

LOCAL SAYING
Sent in by Alfred Froom

When cold winds blow from mountain top,
Mother's puddings limply drop.

LETTER TO THE EDITOR

Dear Sir,

My name is Russell Bleach and I am seven years old. My father knows I am writing but this letter is from me, not him. After reading the Children's Corner column in your 'new-look' magazine for the last three months, I would like to say what I think about it by making up my own word-search game, just as Aunt Audrey did in the January issue. I am enclosing it with my letter. There is a delicious little secret hidden away in my game as well, just like Aunt Audrey's, but as I am only seven I expect it will be much easier to find. I have written a helpful little list of words as well, but they are jumbled up to make the game more fun. If you put them together in the right order they make a sentence for us all, but especially Aunt Audrey, to enjoy.

CHILDREN	WITH	LITTLE
AUDREYS	GAMES	OUT
PATRONISING	STINKS	AUNT
BUTT	INSULTING	SO

WORD SEARCH

N	O	Q	S	F	E	Y	T	M	O	G	B
I	K	L	D	G	M	P	I	S	N	R	O
L	L	N	N	E	R	D	L	I	H	C	K
D	S	I	T	C	P	E	S	S	Y	S	E
A	G	N	T	O	W	I	T	H	S	E	R
W	E	S	Q	T	N	G	I	O	K	M	N
R	K	U	Z	O	L	N	N	L	D	A	L
B	F	L	R	A	U	E	K	P	U	G	S
N	V	T	N	U	A	T	S	D	I	O	B
S	A	I	J	V	T	Y	R	N	F	Z	O
P	H	N	I	U	P	E	J	I	A	V	R
L	A	G	B	M	Y	V	O	W	P	E	S

By the way, Aunt Audrey was quite right when she said that my dear little brother would be standing at my elbow hoping to be allowed to join in with my important, grown-up seven-year-old games, and it was only when I actually used my elbow on him that he cleared off. So, thanks for the tip, Aunt Audrey.

Russell

41

MIRACLES EXPLAINED

(2) The healing of two blind men.

Then he touched their eyes and said, "According to your faith will it be done to you," and their sight was restored. Jesus warned them sternly, "See that no-one knows about this."

Matthew 9 : 29-30

The clue to what was really going on in this jolly account seems to me to lie in the command that no-one should be told what had happened.

My recent research indicates fairly conclusively that these two men were members of an obscure Judean religious group, the name of which can be most accurately translated as 'Grabbers of Jehovah in the Dark'. The central religious ceremony of this group, symbolic, one assumes, of man's desire to reach out and touch Jehovah in a spiritual sense, consisted of a symbolic ritual in which two blindfolded men sought to touch each of the other members of the group in turn within a small, defined area, rather as in the modern children's game of Blind-Man's Buff.

From each generation of this little-known sect, two male children were chosen to be blindfolded at birth and have their blindfolds ritually renewed in a dark place whenever they needed enlarging or replacing because of wear. These two 'Jehovah Catchers', as they

came to be called, lived in a secluded place, and were never allowed to know that there was an alternative to their blindfolded state.

During his years as a travelling fish circus proprietor, Jesus would, without question, have encountered this mysterious group, and acquired a deep understanding of their ways, including the secrets of the 'Jehovah Catchers'. It now seems clear that it was just such a pair of men that Jesus 'healed' on this occasion. As he touched their eyes he explained all the facts that had been withheld from them until now, encouraged them to have faith in the future, and then simply took their blindfolds off! When he said, "See that no-one knows about this," he was, of course, actually saying, "Look, when you tell the world about this, there's no need to mention the blindfolds."

For me, the real miracle is not about restored sight, but about the thorough way in which Jesus had acquired intimate knowledge of local religious customs in preparation for his ministry.

WASH YOUR DIRTY LINEN WITH SIMON BLEACH

Q. Dear Simon Bleach,

I write in connection with the 'verse' that appeared beneath the title of the March edition of The Skull. I am appalled. Imagine how deeply embarrassed and humiliated George Pain's poor Great Aunt must have felt on learning that the whole world is aware of her problems with flatulence?

Maude

A. Dear Maude,

You miss the point. Do you not think that embarrassment caused by revelations of flatulence must pale into insignificance beside the thought of everybody knowing that one is any sort of relative of George Pain's?

Simon

Q. Dear Simon,

I've just been watching that programme on television where that man hypnotises people and they end up doing stupid things that they wouldn't do if they weren't being hypnotised. It's wrong! I know it's wrong, Simon. Whatever they say about helpful therapy and all that it's just wrong and someone ought to jolly well put a stop to it. I've always thought hypnotism is wrong and this has just confirmed it. You agree, don't you? You must do! Hypnotism is definitely -

Philip Jaws

A. Dear Philip,

Sle-e-e-e-p....

Simon

Q. Dear Simon Bleach,

No-one who writes to you ever seems bothered about the kind of secular issues that Christians should be thinking about. Take fishing, for instance. So called 'sports' like fox-hunting are bad enough, but what is your view on the way we feed ourselves with living creatures from the rivers and the seas? Ask yourself this. What sort of state would you be in if you were a herring that had just been caught?

Hilda

A. Dear Hilda,

Gutted.

Simon

A LIMERICK ABOUT OUR VICAR

Sent in by 'a well-wisher - if I could find one...'

An aggressive old vicar called Smedley,
Proclaimed, "With a rifle I'm deadly!
I'll ring one church bell
For a quid, and - oh, hell,
For a fiver I'll play you a medley."

ANNOUNCEMENT

THE PEOPLE OF GENTLY DOWN IN GENERAL, AND THE EDITOR OF THIS MAGAZINE IN PARTICULAR, WISH TO CONGRATULATE STANLEY, A MUSICIAN (ONE HALF OF THE SUPERB MUSICAL DUO 'STANLEY'N'GEORGE') AND MARY, A DOCTOR, ON THEIR RECENT WEDDING. MAY THE FOLLOWING LINES BE OF USE TO THEM AS THE YEARS GO BY.

When he's ruining discussion with
    obsessional percussion,
And an early deafness seems your only
    hope,
When he's piping tunes he stole from some
    half-forgotten Pole,
And he does it on your favourite
    stethoscope,
Forgive, just forgive, as long as you live,
Pass your righteous fury through the
    heavenly sieve,
And forgive.

When you're poking through the stew that
    Mary's placed in front of you,
And you have a bad attack of
    heebie-jeebies,
As you hear her clearly say she's been in
    surgery today,
And you fear you may be looking at the
    freebies,
Forgive, just forgive, as long as you live,
Pass your righteous fury through the
    heavenly sieve,
And forgive.

When he's planning for a tour, but the
    music's sounding poor,
And he's so immersed you wish you'd
    never wed,
When he starts to rave and curse about no
    time left to rehearse,
And you find young George between you in
    the bed,
Forgive, just forgive, as long as you live,
Pass your righteous fury through the
    heavenly sieve,
And forgive.

When she's pinched your pipes of Pan for
    making patterns on a flan,
And your keyboard for her ironing yet
    again,
When she thinks a little kiss'll reconcile
    you to your whistle,
Being used to decongest the outside drain,
Forgive, just forgive, as long as you live,
Pass your righteous fury through the
    heavenly sieve,
And forgive.

When the morning's so confused by the
    instruments he's used,
That the bag you want is not the one
    you get,
And a patient later cries, "Why are you
    looking in my eyes,
Through what seems to be a
    tenor clarinet?"
Forgive, just forgive, as long as you live,
Pass your righteous fury through the
    heavenly sieve,
And forgive.

Should she graciously consent to attend at
    an event,
Where your music flies each heart up
    like a dove,
And her bleeper's ghastly sound brings
    them crashing to the ground,
And you want to pull her entrails out
    - in love,
Forgive, just forgive, as long as you live,
Pass your righteous fury through the
    heavenly sieve,
And forgive.

HELLO EVERYBODY!

A greeting to the parish from **Christine Fitt**, *who is the vicar's secretary, a major pest, I'm sure we would all agree*

I really do want to thank the editor of The Skull for allowing me this little space to introduce myself to people in the parish of St. Yorick's. My name is Christine Fitt, I have been the vicar's secretary since January, and I was very pleased to take up this post, especially as I had previously applied for so many positions without success that I was on the point of giving up. To be honest, I was sure that the Reverend Harcourt-Smedley would also turn me down when I arrived for interview at the wrong time on the wrong day in the wrong parish and forgot to bring references with me, but from the moment when the vicar first set eyes on me in the St. Yorick's vestry when I got there at last he seemed very positive, although he did say and do some rather puzzling things in the course of our encounter.

One of his questions towards the end of the interview, for instance, was, "May I assume that you are unlikely to emulate your predecessors by rushing off to become pregnant at the first possible opportunity?"

Then, before I had a chance to reply to this quite reasonable question, he stared right into my face and muttered, more to himself than to me, "No, no, this one would be likely to receive the bulk of an Iberian downpour."

Try as I might, I am quite unable to comprehend the meaning of that statement, but the vicar smiled as he said it, and I cannot but think it must have been a compliment. Reverend Harcourt-Smedley then went on to tell me that his last three secretaries had stayed for very unsatisfactorily short periods of time before leaving for various reasons connected with marriage or babies.

A short silence ensued at this point, and I became aware that my potential employer was staring even more fixedly at my general appearance, and particularly my face. I was, as usual, wearing my hair in a tidy bun and I had on my working spectacles which are possibly more practical than decorative. He frowned worriedly and said, again more to himself than to me, "Hmm, I seem to recall feature films in which such looks are suddenly..." Then, to me, "Would you oblige me by standing for a moment, please, Miss Fitt?"

I stood obediently and waited as he walked around the desk until he was standing directly in front of me. Then he reached forward and took out the pins from my hair so that it fell around my face. Finally, he removed my spectacles and laid them on the desk behind him. Drawing back his head he studied me for a moment or two, then smiled, shook his head and said, "No, not in this case..."

After that I was offered the post of secretary, and with a feeling of great elation, I turned to leave and walked straight into the vestry toilet, where I felt obliged to remain for a few moments before I emerged, regained my spectacles, and bid farewell once more to the vicar.

I hope to get to know many of you over the months and (dare I say) years to come.

NOTICEBOARD

On Maundy Thursday it is hoped that the church will be packed to the doors for a rendering of Saint Matthew's Passion by the massed male choirs of the Gently Down churches, who have been rehearsing for some weeks now. The dedication of the various choirs to the pursuit of excellence in this project may be measured by their willingness to have some members removed in order that a better sound might be obtained.

EASTER SERVICE

The joint Easter service this year will take place at 10 : 00 a.m. on Sunday April 6th. The vicar has asked me to say that he recently visited an elderly ex-theatrical person who lives beside the church and is too bed-ridden to attend services. This gentleman expressed the hope that our singing on Easter Sunday would be loud enough to be heard from his bedroom. So come on, folks, let's forget our petty troubles for an hour in church and really raise that ancient old poof with our singing. Hallelujah! We are free indeed! Please do not allow children to bring unwrapped chocolate eggs this year. Pew-smearing is not funny, especially for those who have to clean up afterwards.

Our special Good Friday service will be held on err Good Friday in the church hall at 6 : 30 p.m. during which we shall be meditating on err Good Friday, and praying about the things that happened on - the things that happened then.

THE LADIES CIRCLE

meeting will be held once again at Mrs. Tyson's house, 36, Butterwick Avenue, on Thursday the 17th of April at 7 : 00 p.m. This month the Reverend Richard Harcourt-Smedley will be our special guest, speaking on the subject 'The joy of entering heaven'. The vicar has indicated that he is unlikely to be accompanied by his wife on this occasion.

CHILDREN'S CORNER

We are, of course, deeply grateful to 'Aunt Audrey Pellet' for her three lively contributions to our children's corner, but it is possible to have too much of a good thing, so we are now resting her for a spell. This month we welcome Orel Spigget, an American, an evangelist and a newcomer to our parish, who has volunteered to take over the children's corner for the next few months. Ed.

I really want to *thank* Pastor Pilcher for allowing me the opportunity to share my ministerial gifts with the children of the Yorick's parish in *this* way! *Yes I do!* I think you will understand very quickly the kind of impact I have had on the children of America and why so *many* in that *great country* thought it would be *good* for me to leave there and come to this foreign land.

Our theme for this issue is *thanksgiving!* Now, children, I want you to think carefully about the *meaning* of thanksgiving. Did you know that literally, from the original Greek, it means to *give thanks*? Do you remember to *give thanks* for the many blessings you have? I will bet you do *not!* Why not? Unfortunately, we let life's little traps *sink* us into a mire of *hard-heartedness!* We get *caught up* in our petty squabbles and problems. Maybe you do not give thanks because you are having a *difficult time* in school, or because your friends do not like you, or maybe your *dog* was run over by a *car!* Children, that is *no reason not to give thanks!* There are people who have had worse happen to them.

Take Job, who appears in *the book of Job.* He was a *righteous* man, but Satan went to God and said Job was righteous *only* because he had a *big* family and a *lot* of wealth. God got in an *argument* with Satan and finally Satan said he would *prove it!* So Satan marched right out and took away all of Job's property and *killed all of Job's children!* Then he put a lot of *pus-filled sores* all over Job's body and made him sit in ashes. Then he made Job's wife and friends talk him nearly to *death!* Did Job curse God? Was Job still thankful? *Read your Bible* and see for yourself. More important, if you were Job, would you be thankful? Stop and think about it *right now!* Maybe at this very moment God and Satan are watching you, trying to decide whether to take away all you have and *kill your family* just to see if you *will give thanks!* Young Christian boy, young Christian girl, *what* will be your response? Will you say, *Yes!* I will be thankful no matter what! Or will you be an old sourpuss and cause Satan to do *terrible things* to you?

Think it over, young person, and the next time you feel like complaining, *give thanks instead!*

48

14p

THE SKULL

The Parish Magazine of St Yorick's, Gently Down **MAY**

IN MAY I BUILD UP QUITE A THIRST
MY BIRTHDAY'S ON THE TWENTY-FIRST

FAITH IN ACTION

'This people draweth nigh unto me with their mouth . . .'

MATTHEW 15 v8 AV

VICAR : THE REVEREND RICHARD HARCOURT-SMEDLEY D.D. TEL : 569604
CURATE : THE REVEREND CURTIS WEVRAMOL B.D. TEL : 563957
CHURCHWEIRDEN : MISTER C. VASEY B.A. TEL : 563749
VICARIOUS SECRETARY : CHRIS FITT C.T.A.B. TEL : 569604
SKULL CONTRIBUTIONS TO HENRY PITCHER 3, FOXGLOVE ROAD: 563328

A Letter from the Vicar

*As the vicar has been on holiday, this month's letter is
written by Curtis, the curate.*

Hi, everybody!

Curtis here.

Never really done this kind of thing
before, but I thought I'd just tell you all
about something that happened to me the
other day. You see, I had to travel from
Gently Down up to London during the
rush-hour to visit a relative in hospital, and
it involved a short tube journey at the end.
Actually, I'd had to do the same trip the
week before, and it had been horrendously
crowded then with people trying to get to
their various places of work. I'm jolly glad
I don't have to do it every day! Anyway, on
this particular morning it was even worse.
There'd been a work-to-rule by train crews
or something, so the bit round the ticket
barriers was a great sea of commuters,
each waiting to be a sort of small drop of
the next wave allowed down the escalators
to platforms on the lower levels. As I went
down the steps from the mainline station

the sight of all those people stranded yet
again behind the barriers had the same
cramping effect on the muscles of my
stomach as it had the week before.

And yet, this time, something was
definitely different.

Last week there'd been a loud angry
buzz, a feeling that tempers were barely
controlled. Today, there was a different,
calmer atmosphere - and a distinctly different noise. One voice was raised above all
the others, a shrill, enraged voice that
swore and screamed without stopping.
Looking over the heads of the crowd (there
are some advantages to being a fairly tall
curate) I saw that, on the other side of the
barrier, one of the commuters, a shortish,
well-dressed man in his mid-forties,
seemed to have finally cracked up. With
three or four London Underground staff in
wary, circling attendance, he was letting
out all his anger and frustration with complete abandonment. He reminded me a bit
of those characters you see in the silent
comedy films who jump vertically up and
down like small children, shaking their
fists wildly and not really terribly convinc-
ingly, the difference being that I was
entirely convinced by this exhibition. The
person who was providing the cabaret for
his fellow-commuters on this particular
morning was so deeply upset, presumably
by having his travelling plans thwarted,
that he'd lost all control. Tears of sheer
fury ran down his face as he bounced and

raged and roared. It was like seeing a grown-up who'd been stripped of his adulthood to reveal a kid having a very bad tantrum.

What I particularly wanted to tell you about was the effect this had on everyone else. It was fascinating. For a start there was something to look at and listen to as we all waited to be allowed forward. A few people laughed at what was going on, others just stared. But the overwhelming feeling spreading through the crowd was one of relief and a sort of relaxation. That one wild character over there was openly expressing the pent-up frustrations of the rest of us, and the cathartic effect was quite remarkable. In some strange, primitive way justice had been done. A single representative had saved all those present from making fools of themselves by doing it for them.

I noticed one or two of the commuters shaking their heads at the man's behaviour in that slow, arrogantly condemning way that you see car drivers do sometimes when they see learners or idiots like me make mistakes on the road. And it was then that I suddenly remembered another, much more famous time when passers-by shook their heads in exactly the same way as they passed a man who seemed to them to be making an even greater fool of himself.

As the barriers opened and I got swept towards the escalator, I realised that what I'd just seen was quite a powerful little parable. Thought I'd pass it on to you.

Thanks for putting up with me - cheers for now!

Curtis

A PRAYER FOR THE MONTH
By Cissy Booth, aged seven

god i want to pray that my favrit lamb binky from our farm will go to hevven and be with us all after we die i think he will becos i have eaten him so he is inside me like jesus some bits of him are inside a sorted uther members of our fammily but pleese will you put him back together when you get all the bits in it will be a bit of a jig saw puzzel but i know you can do it dont bother with the one called frank becos he allways butted me with his head amen.

LOCAL SAYING

Sent in by Velma Cumbersome

You can't make little delicate porcelain ornaments out of a pile of rotting cabbage on a pitch-black stormy night with thick woollen gloves on.

OBITUARY

Grant Soames
~ died Monday April 20th ~

Grant Soames was not one of those people who forever restlessly strain and strive. Indeed, he rejected the protestant work ethic with a determined and ingenious consistency that really was quite remarkable. Never allowing his attitude to official institutions to become one of petty and churlish independence, Grant placed an extremely high value on that which government agencies were able to offer him, and it was with whole-hearted and humble acceptance that, for most of his life, he collected it every Thursday.

Grant's was not an attractiveness of the immediate, skin-deep variety. No, it was buried deep, deep, deep down inside, like gold in an abandoned mine, so deep in fact that none of us ever quite managed to excavate it. He was not a man who courted cheap, instant popularity. Knowing, for instance, that it is more blessed to give than to receive, Grant steadfastly and committedly insisted that others should avail themselves of that blessing, particularly in the local public house, where his concern for others manifested itself in blunt refusal to ever selfishly snatch an opportunity to buy someone else a drink. Grant was a man of convictions - too many to list here.

Grant infected (Surely affected? Ed.) the area in which he lived. Close neighbours recall him as a man who, by providing a pungently clear focus of attention, was directly responsible for bringing about a stronger sense of unity among those who lived in the vicinity of his home, the dramatic culmination of that unifying process being the presentation of a petition to the council.

For many years Grant's mother and father lived only two streets away from him. If Grant had been a different kind of man, they could so easily have found the dignity and independence of their old age eroded by the continual, smothering presence of an over-protective son. Not so with Grant, whose sensitivity in this area was such that he fastidiously avoided visiting his parents unless he wanted *them* to give something to *him*, a sacrifice the cost of which we can only guess at.

At church Grant was well known as a person who always put himself last, and particularly when a need for volunteers arose, Grant once again generously allowing others to enjoy the chance to serve before even contemplating the idea of pushing himself forward.

Grant died, much as he lived, in a drunken brawl outside The Burglar's Rest. In losing him many of us will feel a sense of personal loss, minor loans never now to be repaid, small items abstracted by Grant from our homes in the course of a visit, and later pawned.

Grant Soames is no longer with us, but his legacy remains, not the usual crude financial one, except in a negative sense, but that priceless legacy of enabling all with whom he came in contact, however wretched, to feel just a little better about themselves.   GRAHAM LETTERWORTH

WASH YOUR DIRTY LINEN WITH SIMON BLEACH

Q. Dear Simon,

My ambition is to be like that man who writes hymns and choruses that are sung in churches all over the country, or even the world. I've written lots already, but I'm not sure what I should do with them now. I wondered if you might have a few ideas. I thought it might help if I showed you a sample of my work. This is the first part of a chorus with actions and props that I've been working on, just to give you a flavour of what I do. It's called **'We Want To Have God.'**

WE WANT TO HAVE
GOD IN OUR THINKING
(I point to my head when I sing this line)
AND GOD IN OUR FEET
(I indicate both of my feet)
GOD IN OUR BLINKING
(I blink really hard and point at my eyes)
AND GOD IN OUR MEAT
(I pick up a real joint of lamb or beef with one hand and point to it with the other)
WE WANT TO BE SALT
TO OUR NEIGHBOURS
(I pick up a large salt container with my free hand and pretend to shake it all over the congregation)
TRUE BRANCHES OF THE VINE
(A helper drapes plastic vines over my shoulders from behind)
A NEW WAVE OF THE SPIRIT
(Humour here - I put the other things down and wave a large bottle of whisky slowly to and fro with one hand above my head - wave of the spirit, see?)
TO GIVE THIS LAND A SIGN
(With my free hand I hold up a large, orange traffic cone to show that we are on the move, but in a controlled and guided way)

That's only the first bit, and it goes on for another four verses with different actions and objects each time. Based on this example, could you give me your candid opinion on whether I ought to go for it, and what I ought to do next. I know some people don't genuinely mean it when they say they want an honest opinion, but I really, really do want you to say exactly what you think. If you reckon it has possibilities just say so, and that will be great, but if you're not impressed, don't waste words, just come right out with it and say it's a load of rubbish, and that will be that.

Mike

A. Dear Mike,
It's a load of rubbish.
Simon

● ● ● ● ● ● ● ● ● ● ● ● ● ●

Q. Dear Simon,

I went to a big Christian conference on the south coast recently, seeking strength and motivation to do something really useful for God. While I was there some of the brothers and sisters surrounded me for more than two hours and marinaded me in prayer. As a result of this experience I think I might be ready to serve. What do you think?

Robert

A. Dear Robert,
Yes, with a little light seasoning and five minutes under the grill I'm quite sure you will be quickly consumed for the Lord.
Simon

AN ALPHABETICAL

A is for Anglican ladies in hats,
   B is for Belfries where Bishops Breed Bats,
C is for Candles and Chapels and Choirs,
   Curates, Commissioners,
   Crooked Church spires, Crosses, Collections,
   And Change for the better,
D is for Damn that vain previous letter,
   E is for Everyone does what he wants,
F is for Funerals, Follies, and Fonts,
   G is for God and for Graveyard as well,
H is for Heaven and Heating and Hell,
   I is for Icons and Inter-church whist,
J is for Jenkins (who may not exist),
   K is for Kingdom, the King and his search,
L is for Leaving his Lambs in the Lurch,
   M is for Matins and Mass and Modernity,

ANGLICAN POEM

N is for Notices reaching eternity,

O is for Outreach and sowing the seed,

P is for Praise which we don't seem to need,

Q is for Quiet-time (see the above),

R is for Raising the Roof with our love,

S is for Sin and Surprise and Salvation,

Synods and Sexual Orientation,

Suffering, Sadness, Sermons and Smells,

T is for Time and the Tolling of bells,

U is for Unity, one with another,

V is for Vicars who'd rather not bother,

W stands for a World in decline,

X is for Xmas, a promising sign,

Y is for Yobs and Youth fellowships too,

Z is for all of us, Z is for Zoo.

By Adam Booth

NIGEL & CAROLINE ASHBY
By Henry King

It is time for my third Spotlight interview. I feel like a seasoned reporter now. My notebook has got things written in it and one of my biros is a bit chewed at one end. This month I am visiting the Ashby family who live on the new estate behind the even newer supermarket where the market used to be. I arrive at number twenty-four Chisholm Avenue at exactly four o'clock on Saturday, which is the time I arranged with Nigel Ashby last week.

As I stand still to check the house number for a moment, I hear, coming from inside the house, the distant sounds of singing and something that might be a tambourine being played.

IMPRESSED
Passing through a wooden gate that has a notice on it saying 'THIS IS THE LORD'S HOUSE SO IT'S YOURS TOO', I find myself in a very neat front garden with flowers growing tidily in well weeded beds. The whole house looks as if it has only just been unpacked. When a little boy of about eight comes to the door in answer to my knock, he looks as if he has only just been unpacked as well. He is dressed mainly in white and, as far as I can see, totally clean.

I say, "Good afternoon, are your mummy or daddy at home, please?"

The little boy says, "Welcome to our house. You must be Mr. King. My name is Anthony. My mother and father are expecting you. Please come in and I'll tell them that you're here."

RADIO 4
Deeply impressed, I follow Anthony through an immaculate hall into one of those longish sitting-rooms that has been formed by knocking two rooms into one. Nigel and Caroline Ashby and two girls who must be their daughters are sitting in a rough circle. Nigel has a guitar, while each of the others is holding a songbook, and has an opened bible nearby. One of the daughters is holding the tambourine that I heard just now when I was outside.

When they see me come through the sitting-room door it is as if the most wonderful person in the whole universe has dropped in unexpectedly. Nigel puts his guitar aside immediately and, jumping to his feet, comes over and pumps my hand vigorously. He has one of those faces that seems able to convey warmth through one eye, and responsible concern through the other. His voice is resonant but warm like someone on Radio 4.

"Henry!" he says. "Really, really good to see you, mate. We've just finished family worship time. Cass and I have been looking forward to your visit all day, haven't we, Cass?"

THRILLED
Caroline Ashby is very attractive but obviously also a grown-up. When she smiles at me, it is as if life is unable to offer her anything much more satisfying than my scintillating presence. Her eyes look as if she has answers to everything. I find myself wishing that I could sit on her lap and be cuddled by her while I tell her my little secrets.

"Henry," she says, "the girls have been dying to meet you. This is Ruth, she's thirteen, and this is our lovely biggest girl, Mary, and she's sixteen."

The girls are very pretty and pure looking. They smile brilliantly and do little charming waves at me. They do actually appear to be absolutely thrilled to see me. I cannot think why.

"The girls are very cross with us," says Nigel, "because we've said that they can't be in for the interview."

I look at the daughters. These girls are not cross. They are giggling at their father's playfulness. I do not think these girls get cross very often. Caroline says that the girls have been fighting over who should be allowed to be the one to make me a drink, and that Mary is the winner. Mary is so concerned and attentive in her desire to know if I would like a drink, and, if so, exactly what kind of drink I would like, that I become a little tongue-tied. In the end I gracefully accept, and ask for a coffee. Everyone nods, seeming to regard this as an incredibly wise choice.

DEPRIVED

While Mary disappears with her mother into the kitchen, I am urged by Nigel to sit in what is obviously the most comfortable armchair in the room. Thirteen-year-old Ruth comes and sits close to me on the arm of my chair as though I have been a favourite uncle for years. When she listens to me speak her eyes are so clear and trusting that I desperately wish I was the kind of adult that she must think all adults are because of the kind of adults she must have been brought up by, if you see what I mean. Anthony sits symmetrically in a chair opposite us, exuding boyish charm and appropriate social restraint.

Eventually, my coffee comes and the children file out politely, reluctant though they apparently are to be deprived of my fascinating company. There are just Nigel and Caroline and myself left in the room. I cannot bring myself to call her Cass. I just can not. I take out my notebook and a pen. Nigel and Caroline are leaning forward in their chairs, both wearing frowns of keen expectancy, total co-operation and undiluted willingness. I feel a bit silly. I read my first question.

PUZZLED

I say, "Nigel and Caroline, you are famous at St. Yorick's for hosting the Parish Weekend, and greeting people at the door each Sunday, and leading midweek groups and all that sort of thing. When did you first realise that you had this gift of hospitality - of looking after other people?"

Nigel looks genuinely puzzled. He says, "Well. it's very nice of you to say all those things, Henry, but we really don't do all that much, do we, Cass? Well, Cass does." He takes his wife's hand affectionately. "Cass has a real gift for picking up hurt folk and getting them moving again, don't you, darling?"

Caroline says, "We've been so very fortunate, Henry. The Lord has given us the great privilege of coming into contact with quite a lot of hurting people so that we can be just a very small link in the chain of his loving concern for them. We're constantly amazed that he uses us, aren't we, Nigel?"

Nigel nods and says, "I can see that the Lord has great plans for you as well, Henry. What sort of direction is he leading you in?"

I look at their faces. They really want to know. Caroline is looking at me as if the whole of her future happiness depends on hearing my answer to Nigel's question. I want to fall into her eyes and be safe there.

IMPULSE

I reply rather feebly, "Well, I did sort of hope - and think - that, well, that it might be possible for me to be a sort of journalist. That's why I - that's why I volunteered to do this Spotlight thing."

Nigel and Caroline react to this thin statement of hope with little gasps of smiling wonderment and nods of seriously considered approval.

Nigel says, "Well, it really is an honour for us to be part of the beginning of your career, Henry, mate. We shall never forget this, shall we, Cass?"

Caroline nods and smiles so warmly at me that I feel like rolling over on my back on the floor in front of her with my feet and hands in the air just to be close to her. Thank God, I resist the impulse.

She says, "When you're a famous reporter, Henry, doing wonderful things for God, we'll remember that we were two of the first people you ever talked to. We shall be very proud."

My next question isn't on my list, but I can't help asking it. It just bursts out. "Why is it that you - both of you - are like you are, all nice and happy with nice children and a clean house and having worship times and thinking everyone else is wonderful and all that, and most people aren't. I mean, why doesn't God make all Christians like you?"

For an instant the Ashbys stare at me open-mouthed, then they both burst into laughter. After a moment or two Nigel wipes his eyes and says, "You're going to make a great journalist if you carry on asking questions like that, Henry old mate. Really took us aback for a bit there." He looks at Caroline, who nods very gently. When Nigel speaks again he sounds very serious.

"Look, Henry, that's an important question, so I'm going to answer it properly, and I'm not going to be silly. It's not quite as wonderful or as easy as it looks, but you're right. We have been very lucky with our marriage and our children and all that sort of thing, and when I use the word 'lucky' I'm not being ungrateful to God.

MEDAL

He looks after the most important part of us all the time, but a lot of it's about the way we're made. I think we would have had a pretty good marriage even if we hadn't been Christians. Now, the real heroes, the ones who deserve to get a great big medal when they get to Heaven, are the people who have to battle all the time against who or what they are or what they're suffering from, and still go on following Jesus. We know some real fighters. We meet them all the time, and we really admire them. Cass and me have got a lot, so a lot's going to be expected from us. See what I mean?"

I leave a few minutes later with the whole family waving furiously at me as I walk down the garden path. They make me feel like a star.

St. Yorick's is lucky to have the Ashbys, however accidental they are.

NOTICEBOARD

SERVICES

SUNDAY
8:00 a.m. Holy Communion
9:30 a.m. Family Circus
11:00 a.m. Moaning Prayer
6:30 p.m. Evening Prayer

WEDNESDAY
10:30 a.m. Holy Continuum

Hello, good people, Dave Billings here. I know it must seem ridiculously early, but after last year's fiasco I thought I'd put out a really early reminder that lots of people will be wanting to take part in the Harvest Supper Entertainment later this year (loads of people have told me they're going to do something really special this time), so don't hang about - get your names to me as soon as you possibly can and I'll make sure you're down on the list. I'm looking for comics, musicians, actors, jugglers, dancers - the more the merrier! Look forward to hearing from you, folks!

Catch me at church or ring me on 568074.

Reverend Harcourt-Smedley asked me to ensure that an extract from Bishop Stanley's address is printed in this month's edition of The Skull. No doubt he is hoping that some of us will write to the bishop to express our appreciation of his visit in April. Here is the address. I give it in full, as an extract might not ensure safe arrival:

Bishop Stanley Purley,
Trinity House, Cathedral Lane,
Wexford. LM22 3CV

I am quite sure that the bishop would be grateful for the inclusion of a stamped, addressed envelope if a reply is required. **Miss C. Fitt, Church Secretary.**

THE LADIES CIRCLE

will meet on Thursday May 15th at Mrs. Tyson's house in Butterwick Avenue. This month Mrs. Burwick will be giving us expert tips on how to make our legs more beautiful. It will also be a Bring and Shave evening.

All are welcome to attend at the church hall on Saturday May 24th, when a dramatic rendering of the coming of The Holy Spirit at Pentecost in the upper room will be presented by members of the church. The evening, devised, written and directed by Victor Clements, begins at 7:30 p.m., and promises to be something very unusual, although Victor is refusing to give anything specific away. Hot and cold drunks will be served after the play.

The second P.C.C. of the year will take place at the vicarage on Thursday May 8th at 7 30. The vicar wishes it to be known that he is fully aware of the football fixture that coincides with this occasion. Please bear in mind that edited highlights of the P.C.C. meeting will not be available later in the evening.

THE YOUTH CLUB

will meet at 6 : 00 p.m. on Friday June 30th behind the church for a special half-term outing. The local fire-service has generously offered to show us around the station. Be warned, though, if the alarm sounds all we are likely to see is several people sliding rapidly down the pope! Don't miss this very unusual opportunity.

CHILDREN'S CORNER
BY OREL SPIGGETT

_Hi!_ Today's message applies to _parents and children!_

Last Sunday morning _during_ the service, there were two _unruly_ children sitting _directly behind me!_ I turned a stern look upon them, but, friends, they _smirked_ at me and they _laughed_ at me and they continued to _giggle and whisper_ behind _my_ back. When I was a boy such behaviour would have resulted in me being _dragged outside_, given a _stern lecture_ and a _sound spanking!_ Alas, such a response _does not occur_ in these wild days. I have met the parents of these children and I _know them_ to be part of that new _liberal breed_ which regards discipline as a four-letter word! But _what does God think?_ Is our God a namby-pamby parent who is afraid to _chastise_ his wayward children? My bible says, _no, he is not!_ God _dealt with_ the children of Israel in the following way. He left them to wander in the desert for _forty years_. Friends, He allowed neighbouring nations to attack them, conquer them and _sell them into slavery_. Yes, He did! He sent _diseases_ upon them and let parts of their bodies _fall off_. Friends, He let them _die_ in their miserable sins. Why? Because He _loved_ them. That is _discipline!_ That is how parents _should be_ with their children. Children of the church, understand that if your parents love you they _will discipline you in just such a way!_ And, if you still fail to take that discipline to heart, _remember_ the words of Deuteronomy 21:

If someone has a stubborn and rebellious son who will not obey his father and mother, who does not heed them when they discipline him, then his father and mother shall take hold of him and bring him out to the elders of his town at the gate of that place... Then all the men of the town shall stone him to death.

So long! I shall be _watching you_ next Sunday!

60

14p

THE SKULL

The Parish Magazine of St Yorick's, Gently Down　　　JUNE

JUST BEFORE THE END OF JUNE
WE KNOW JULY IS COMING SOON

FAITH IN ACTION

'. . .and drawing nigh
unto the ship . . .'

JOHN 6 v19

faith

VICAR : THE REVEREND RICHARD HARCOURT-SMEDLEY D.D. TEL : 569604
CURATE : THE REVEREND CURTIS WEVARMOL B.D. TEL : 563957
CHURCHWEIRDEN : MISTER C. VASEY B.A. TEL : 563749
VICAR'S SECRETARY : CHRISSIE FITT C.T.A.B. TEL : 569604
SKULL CONTRIBUTIONS TO HENRY PITCHER 3, FOXGLOVE ROAD: 563328

A LETTER AND AN APOLOGY FROM THE VICAR

I shower Heaven daily with grateful thanks for the benefits that accrue to me through the work done by Miss Fitt, my secretary, however, one or two words do need to be said about a small misunderstanding that occurred last month. When I requested that our venerable Bishop Stanley's address should be published in the magazine, I was referring, of course, to the sermon that he preached during his last visit, not the name of his street and his post code. Unfortunately (I suppose) there is room for only a very short extract from the bishop's blessedly lengthy and learned message. May God bless it to the hearts of those of us who do not find it uniformly opaque, and may it serve to inflate the already bulging intellect of Miss Fitt.

EXTRACT FROM THE BISHOP'S ADDRESS

'Let your yea be yea, and your nay be nay.'

Matthew 5 : 37

Life is full of opportunities, is it not, to say 'Yea' or to say 'Nay'?

....just this week I was faced with precisely that dilemma when I was asked a question to which, realistically, there were only those two possible answers available. Effectively, I could reply in the affirmative, or I could respond negatively. Two distinct potential trends there, that, because of the blatant oppositeness of their natures, were bound to take me in diametrically opposed directions, depending on which of the two options I selected. And it is indeed this sense of contrast, highlighting the diversity of theoretical resultant consequences, which informs us of the true disparity between the elements of this dual choice that so frequently confronts us. Bringing credibility and integrity to the operation of such a crisis of perception is almost exclusively dependent on the development of validly rational insights into the phenomenology of what we comprehend to be moral or task-oriented plusses and minuses.....

....it is therefore essential that our watchword continues to be 'Simplicity'. Don't you agree?

Let us ensure that our yea be yea and our nay be may. **Amen.**

THE VICAR'S LETTER

Dairy Beloxed,

It seems fitting that I should make some comment on the special Pentecost meeting that was held last month in the church hall. Individual reactions to the extraordinary events of that evening have varied from one extreme to another. A much respected parishioner described the occasion as: "a disgrace, and a permanent disfigurement, not only on the face of local Anglicanism, but on that of the church of Christ in general," whilst George Pain, a parishioner who is respected by nobody at all as far as I am aware, descibed it as "The best free laugh I've had in yonks."

If I had been consulted, which I certainly was not, I might have tentatively supported the broad concept of a production aiming to dramatically portray the gathering of the disciples in the upper room on the day of Pentecost, but I should have most strongly advised against certain specific aspects of the evening. I would, in particular, have definitely expressed reservations concerning the means by which it was planned that the tongues of flame should be portrayed.

Surely it cannot have been less than abundantly clear to just one or two of the supposedly intelligent

continued overleaf.......

PRAYERS FOR THE MONTH
Sent in from all over the parish

For dearest Villum, that sponging may be sufficient... For Elspeth, feeling betrayed, that her hammock might hold... For Douglas, so fastidious, that nothing essential will be removed... For Veronica, that the whole thing may lift, and that shoring up will be a formality... For James and Ben, that higher altitudes will resolve their problem... For Maureen, that fashions may drastically change one day... For Mavis, so patient, that the switching on might happen again very soon... For Daniel, in the grip of meteorology, that one day his vision may be cleared and he will return to his sorrowing family... For Raymond, that he may see velcro in a new light and no longer be afraid... For Winnie, that the blotches may prove to be washable... For Stanley, terrified of his own shoulder-blades, that the running away might cease... For Brian, weary of being constantly weighed... For Pansy, that the crows will thrive, and that a higher fence will be erected...   **Amen**

LOCAL SAYING
Sent in by 'Cordless' O'Leary

First cut, last buttered.

continued from previous page

persons involved, that strapping gas cylinders on to the backs of those depicting the disciples was an act of unparalleled lunacy. I do not understand how any sane human being can have thought it possible for such a large group of 'actors' to not only secretly and simultaneously ignite their cylinders with cigarette lighters, but to do so in such a manner that any normal audience would be happily persuaded that the resultant, very audibly hissing flame appearing above their heads was produced by the Holy Spirit, and not by Calor Gas.

Nevertheless, if this had been the sole problem challenging the success of the project all might still have been reasonably well - faintly absurd, of course, but reasonably well. However, the twin factors of paper head-dresses and a refusal by the organisers of the fiasco to manage without a literal representation of the 'mighty rushing wind' determined that this was not to be so. A sudden, quite violent movement of air, produced by what I believe is known as a wind machine, hired for the night, caused stray fragments from two of the head-dresses to come into close contact with their respective wearers' spurious tongues of flame. The head-dresses were thereby ignited in an abrupt and highly alarming manner. It was at this point, in a moment of startlingly vivid surrealism, that a fireman in full uniform, presumably present in order to deal with just such an accident, strode onto the stage clutching a metallic red cylinder, and proceeded to summarily extinguish the Holy Spirit.

Fortunately, nobody was harmed in this brief conflagration, but one cannot help surmising that if the audience for the evening included folk who were unsure about a decision to commit to the Christian faith, this sad depiction of the early church in a depressed, sodden and quenched state was unlikely to be the spur which would goad them into wholehearted acceptance of Our Lord's teaching. Let us hope that in future less ambitious and more feasible attempts will be made to tell the story of Pentecost.

From the ducks of your verruca,

Riskand Handcount-Seedley.

MIRACLES EXPLAINED

(3) Walking on the water.

During the fourth watch of the night Jesus went out to them, walking on the lake. When the disciples saw him walking on the lake, they were terrified. "It's a ghost," they said, and cried out in fear.

Matthew 14 : 25-26

In this jolliest of stories we return to the historically self-evident fact, mentioned in a previous note, of Jesus' previous career as the proprietor of an itinerant fish circus. I believe it highly likely that the fear felt by the disciples would have been intensified by the phenomenon of Jesus appearing to abruptly speed up and slow down at irregular intervals as he made his progress towards them across the surface of the lake. The reason? Well, what more likely than that he was actually balancing on the back of a large, trained fish, swimming just below the surface of the water, a fish which, although subject to the whims of its master, was unable, by its very nature, to move at a totally consistent speed? As the master neared the boat and became clearly visible he would have commenced a walking-on-the-spot motion, rather in the manner of Marcel Marceau, the great French mime artist. No wonder the disciples were disturbed. What a sight that must have been!

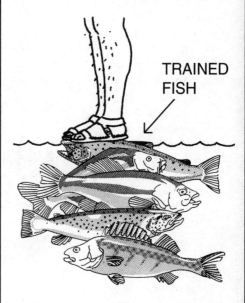

TRAINED FISH

For me, the real miracle lies, not in any magical 'walking on the water', but in the amount of training and practice that must have been necessary to produce such an effect.

A PLACE TO STAY -
CROSSROADS!

A special holiday article written for The Skull and sent to us by Christine Tuttsonson, who works at the new Crossroads Inter-denominational Christian Conference Centre in the very heart of Great Britain

Greetings! It's really great to have a chance to tell you about Crossroads. I've been working here for two months now. I really feel part of it, and I think it's the best place for a holiday or conference I've ever seen (apart from Mum and Dad's B & B at Gently Down, of course!)

At Crossroads we like to think that we are able to cater for members of just about every kind of Christian denomination that you can imagine. Our aim is to suit the guests, whatever their churchmanship might be, and we work very hard to make that possible.

Take Pentecostals and House Church people, for instance. They really seem to appreciate rooms on the Charismatic Floor, where the ceilings are just a little bit higher than usual, and we make sure there are mattresses on the floors as well as on the beds. (Older members of H.T.B. usually opt for the Percy Edwards Suite.) Meals can be taken in the rooftop Rapture Restaurant, but we do ask either that accounts are settled before the meal

begins, or that both diners are in a position to pay. Menus remain the same each day except for the breakfast menu, which is new, every morning it's new. We also have a lounge for people who just want to relax, where seats are always available because it hardly gets used.

Christian Outreach Centre groups, by the way, are offered similar facilities, but with non-optional sound-proofing in all rooms. This facility is also available to 'REFORM' to be cross in.

Baptists often choose to stay with us, perhaps because they know that they will be offered en-suite rooms, featuring baths equipped with walk-down steps, and an automatic wall-speaker rendering of 'Bringing in the Sheaves' each time the hot tap is switched on.

Rooms on the Anglican floor, by contrast, feature only hand-held hair-washing sprays and baby-baths, and can be situated as high or as low in the building as required. We do have a small number of rooms with windows facing in the direction of Rome for Anglo-Catholic visitors. I ought to mention, by the way, that tea and coffee-making facilities are available for the personal use of all non-conformist guests, but Anglican visitors will be served at specially arranged times by the management. In addition, a detailed programme of events for the day is available for those Anglican guests who prefer it. So far the response has been a sort of mumbled monotone.

All Methodist rooms are large enough to accommo-date meetings, meetings about meetings, and meetings about meet-ings about meetings, all at the same time.

A selection of rooms on the ground floor is reserved for members of the United Reformed Church who are unable to negotiate the stairs or work out how to use the lifts.

Calvinistic visitors are very fortunate because, in their case, booking is not necessary, but unlike those groups whose accounts are settled in advance, they will be expected to pay and pay and pay eventually.

We are now also able to accomodate the Jesus Army, since taking on staff with hearing defects who are specially trained to not mind how many times they get converted.

Everybody who works here is particularly proud of our new annexe, isolated from the rest of the establishment with seperate entrances and exits, and specially designed to enable visitors from the Strict and Particular Closed Brethren to feel absolutely sure that they are the only guests in the Conference Centre.

Guests are warmly encouraged to use our hotel laundry service, which guarantees that even striped pyjamas will be automatically washed as white as snow, except in the case of Roman Catholics, who will be asked to make personal requests for the cleaning of each garment at set times during the week. Roman Catholic visitors should also be aware that they may be required to spend a considerable time by the fire in the lobby on arrival before being shown to their rooms.

The indoor heated swimming pool is available for general use, mystics tending to favour the deep end, while the shallow end is reserved for certain fellowships who need to keep their hands free for clapping. American evangelists are always welcome to use the pool, but they are asked to walk in, not on the water.

All in all, our hotel works on a basis of mutual respect and trust. Guests are asked, for instance, not to tip uniformed commissionaires as, more often than not, they are likely to be Salvation Army ofi-cers holding open-air meetings just out-side the front door.

Our newest innovation is the Unity Room, a place where all the guests can mingle freely, whatever their differences. This has not really taken off yet. There is one man who can usually be found in there, but he is neither staff nor guest, and, oddly enough, none of us can quite bring ourselves to ask his business. But then, he does no harm, sitting quietly on his own.

WASH YOUR DIRTY LINEN WITH SIMON BLEACH

Q. Dear Simon,

Don't you think we should be deeply sensitive to spiritual messages given to us in the course of church meetings, even if they are not immediately easy to understand? What, for instance, did you make of that strange, inexplicable but oddly exciting moment during the service in church last Sunday with Curtis the curate in charge, when Earnest Dibling suddenly shouted out in a very loud voice from near the back, for no apparent reason, "Yes, it's in East Anglia, several miles north of Ipswich!"?

Spooky, or what?

William

A. Dear William,

You have failed to take two very important things into consideration. First, Earnest Dibling, in common with most of the other members of his extensive family, has a hearing problem. Secondly, the curate had just pointed out and addressed a question to Philip Jaws who was sitting with his arm raised, immediately behind Earnest Dibling. It was this question that Earnest Dibling completely misheard and, believing that Curtis was pointing directly at him, immediately replied to. Thus, the brief, unintentional, hitherto inexplicable and not very exciting at all dialogue in question took the following form:
CURTIS: *Have you a Word of Knowledge?*
EARNEST: *Yes, I have. I've been there. It's in East Anglia, several miles north of Ipswich.*

You can see how wars start, can't you?

Simon

• • • • • • • • • • • • • •

Q. Dear Simon Bleach,

I am the person who, in good faith, sent you a sample of my songwriting, 'We Want To Have God', a couple of months ago. I read your reply to my letter in last month's Skull with total disbelief. I would be most grateful if you could justify the use of five words as an appropriate response to what I wrote.

Michael G. Strang

A. Dear Michael G. Strang,

No problem, I see your point, and I agree. I can't justify the use of five words. I was, in fact, going to use just one word, but I didn't want to offend other readers and I didn't want you to feel I hadn't taken any trouble.

Simon

• • • • • • • • • • • • • •

Q. Dear Simon,

My name is Graham Clark, and as you and most of the other people at St. Yorick's know - and if you don't, why don't you? - I am the weak incompetent who has lost control of the youth club that meets at least once every month to destroy the church hall. I expect a fair number of your saintly readers are quite surprised to find that I can write at all. After all, it doesn't take much of a brain to occupy twenty or thirty kids for three hours on a week-day evening, especially when one third of the group makes John the Baptist look self-indulgent, one third are Mike Tyson fans and the other third behave like him. The boys are even worse.

Anyway, leaving all that aside, which is what always happens to it, in March the vicar wrote a highly critical and uninformed letter in this magazine about the conduct of the youth club - something about a few miserable scraps of pancake that got dropped, and a childish prank on the noticeboard - and I didn't think it worth replying to, especially as the vicar has never, as far as I am aware (and I would be unlikely to know anything that I do not see with my own eyes because no-one ever bothers to actually inform me of anything) felt it to be part of his ministry to visit the organisation from which the church of the future is to be drawn. Thank God for the curate. He does at least get stuck in!

Anyway, in that same letter, Harcourt-Smedley enthused about the advent of some new group of small children, the members of which were going to teach my crass and evil older children how to live. The likely contribution to be made by these children, or 'little harbingers of heaven', as I believe they were lyrically described, was to be that they would, like little bulbs and buds, begin to sprout and burst and add colour to our lives. Well, I am unable to comment on the extent to which these angelic beings might have sprouted, especially as I have no idea what the process might involve, but what I can bear

witness to, as leader of a group which meets on an evening following the afternoon in which they meet, is that on the last occasion when they met, at least one of them had certainly been doing some bursting - witness the revolting nappy that had been stuffed into a most unexpected crevice.

As for bringing colour into our lives - well, Harcourt-Smedley is a prophet - they have most certainly been doing that. Most of it seems to have come from pots of paint and it has been brought into our lives via chairs, tables, walls, shelves and a number of other surfaces that are in regular use by other hall-users.

I really do hope that whoever is in charge of these little spirits of the springtime will get a grip on the situation, otherwise the older children are likely to be corrupted into believing that they also can do as they please...

Graham Clark

A. Dear Nobby,
Thanks for being willing to share your chips with us all!
Simon

C POETRY CORNER

MY LIFE AND WORK
By H. Tuttsonson

For fifteen years at Willow Grove,
I've done my B & B,
And all that time my husband Sid,
Has been assisting me.
Rooms all come with bath and shower,
Plus 'Sky' with full instructions,
And people coming through the church,
Get generous reductions.
Last Friday week I saw a chance,
I didn't want to miss,
To take my business forward,
And it came about like this.
I said to Sid in bed, "Look, Sid - "
He said, "I beg your pardon?"
I said, "Sid, I've not said it yet,
It's just about the garden,
What about if in the Spring,
As well as B & B's,
We put some tables on the lawn,
And serve up snacks and teas?"
Sid said, "Yeah, I s'pose we could,
But who'd do all the graft?"
He looked at me, I looked at him,
He nodded - how we laughed!
So we began to put on teas,
I'm really glad we did,
The work is never easy,
But thank the Lord for Sid.
If you want tea or B & B,
We'd love to hear from you,
Our number starts with 569,
And ends with 342.

NOTICEBOARD

𝔖𝔢𝔯𝔳𝔦𝔠𝔢𝔰

𝔖𝔲𝔫𝔡𝔞𝔶

8 : 00 a.m. Holy Communion (guns)

9 : 30 a.m. Foamy Service

11 : 00 a.m. Moping Payer

6 : 30 p.m. Evening Prayer

𝔚𝔢𝔡𝔫𝔢𝔰𝔡𝔞𝔶

10 : 30 a.m. Wholly Commission

Dave Billings here, chaps and chapesses! Another reminder that although the jolly old Harvest Supper Entertainment on September 27th is still quite a long way in the future, it would help if I could have just one or two names now to start making up my list for the big evening. Come on, folks, I just know that there's a lot of talent out there, and I want to hear about it. So, let me know on 568074.

Edna Galt, our voluntary and much-valued church hall caretaker and cleaner will be taking a holiday for the first two weeks in July. Volunteers to cover her work while she's away would be very much appreciated. Please contact the curate on 563957 if you feel able to help in this way. Primary responsibility is to maintain well-stacked chars.

Our annual Parish Picnic will take place on Saturday June 14th at Bates Farm. This year Farmer Bates has had his mower out, so we shall not be 'miserably hunting for each other through the long grass', nor 'crawling damply around the banks of the Orinoco', as two people so picturesquely put it last year. Please bring food for one extra person. The vicar will, as in previous years, conclude the event with a short worm.

As many of you know, the Ladies Circle special Fun for the Fundless day will be taking place on July 5th, when a hundred folk from a deprived East End parish will be entertained for a day. The ladies need a lot of food, so hunt through the back of your larders for any of those rusty old tins that will only get thrown away anyway, or those iffy-looking packets of food that have gone too far over their sell-by dates for you to offer them to your family.
Remember, there's a real joy in generous giving.

Make a date in your dairies now for our annual cricket contest between St. Yorick's and Gently Down Pentecostal Church. The match is due to take place at 2 : 00 p.m. on July 19th on the village green, and should be a lot of fun. Contact Brian Wisney at his surgery in the High Street if you would like to take part. He is particularly anxious to find someone who is able to keep wicked without flinching, as we are fortunate to have a demon bowler on our side this year. Also, if enough people fancy a nut one evening, Brian's your man!

The Ladies Circle meets this month in the church hall at 7 : 30 on Thursday June 19th, and takes the form of a talk from German pastor, Helga Durr, who is staying with Mrs. Tuttsonson and hoping to improve her English during a holiday in this country. Pastor Durr has written a short note to the editor in which she says, **'I am surveying the area that confronts me gigantically to existing with you surmounting the evening in query.'**

Dear Mr. Pitcher,

It seems extraordinary to me, in an age when communication skills are supposed to be at their peak, that there can be so many misprinted words in a magazine such as this. In the January issue you assured us that the appointment of your wife as a proof-reader would ensure improvement in this area, but frankly the problem seems as great as ever. If I were to be equally inexact in my leading of the choir or playing of the organ on Sundays there would be complaints enough, I'm sure you would agree. A little more application please!

Herbert Spanning

Dear Mr. Spanning,

My wife has asked me to thank you for your kind and constructive comments on the quality of her proof-reading. She points out that most of the mistakes occur towards the end of each magazine when she has become a little tired after checking the bulk of the copy. She also asked me to say how much she appreciates your contribution to the musical side of church life, and hopes that one as conscientious as you will forgive her foolish lapses, and trust that she will try much harder in future.

It only remains, Herbert, for me to add, that if you ever write a similar letter about my nice forgiving wife again, I shall insert you into the lowest levels of the narrowest pipe on your organ and play Phil and John records at the other end until you scream for mercy. I do hope this is exact enough for you. (N.B. This paragraph not for publication)

Henry Pitcher

FROM THE EDITOR

CALLING ALL CHILDREN!

How would you like to win a special prize of three different kinds of chocolate bar of your choice? You would? Right! Get your colouring pens out and do me a really good picture of the vicar, Mr. Harcourt Smedley. Make sure you get those bushy eyebrows of his right - nice and thick! And don't forget the lovely wobbly bits on his face. Next month I'll publish the best entries and award a prize of three chocolate bars for the winner, two for second, and one for third. The vicar himself has agreed to judge the competition, so that should be interesting, shouldn't it? I'd like to have had a go at it myself. I'm sure you'll do much better, so - away you go!

14p

THE SKULL

The Parish Magazine of St Yorick's, Gently Down   JULY

JULY IS SOMETIMES VERY HOT
BUT WHEN IT ISN'T, IT IS NOT

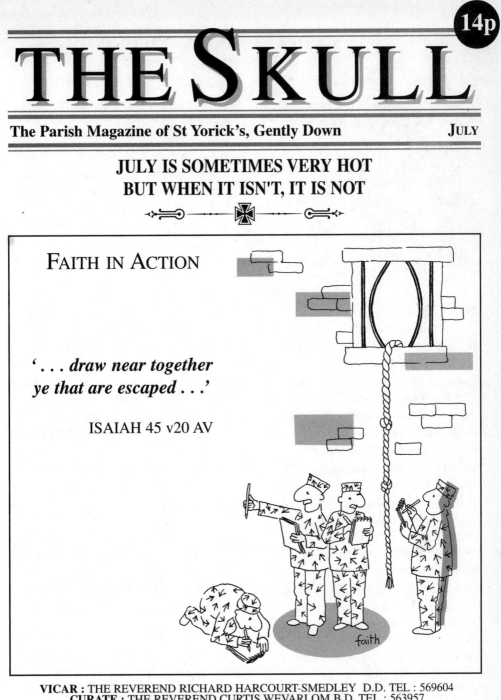

FAITH IN ACTION

'... draw near together
ye that are escaped...'

ISAIAH 45 v20 AV

VICAR : THE REVEREND RICHARD HARCOURT-SMEDLEY D.D. TEL : 569604
CURATE : THE REVEREND CURTIS WEVARLOM B.D. TEL : 563957
CHURCHWEIRDEN : MISTER C. VASEY B.A. TEL : 563749
VICAR'S SECRETARY : CRISPY FITT C.T.A.B. TEL : 569604
SKULL CONTRIBUTIONS TO HENRY PITCHER 3, FOXGLOVE ROAD: 563328

A Letter from the Vicar

Nearly Beloved,

I am well aware that there has been a great deal of loose talk about a particular meeting of the Ladies Circle three months ago in April, to which I was honoured to be invited as the guest speaker. I should like to publicly explain the circumstances which occurred on the evening in question, so that foolish tittle-tattle by those who were not present may be curtailed.

I must begin by saying, in my own defence, that the occupation of clergyman is one that requires a great deal of tact and diplomacy, and it is perhaps inevitable that there will be times when one's ability to, as it were, dovetail with the entire congregation's needs is temporarily non-existent. On that particular morning I was not entirely myself owing to the fact that Elspeth and I had had one of our occasional disagreements concerning an elderly and critical couple in the congregation whose attitude and manner fell, in my estimation, far short of the Utopian ideal, if I may express it in those strong terms, but whom Elspeth regarded as a necessary cross that is bound to accompany all attempts at genuine ministry. As it happens, this devoted couple passed away within a few days of each other in the week that followed, so, within a very short time, Elspeth and I were able to bury our differences.

On the day in question, however, I must confess that, by the time I arrived at Mrs. Tyson's house for the meeting of the Ladies Circle, I had reached a point where my patience was almost exhausted. I did, however, begin by behaving in as jovial a fashion as I could manage. As far as I can recall, the ensuing conversation took the following form:

ME : (SITTING DOWN AND BEAMING AROUND AT THE CIRCLE OF LADIES WHO WERE DRINKING TEA) Well, good evening, ladies. I must say, I could murder a cup of tea...

MRS L.: (REPROACHFULLY FROM MY LEFT) My husband was murdered many years ago, Reverend Harcourt-Smedley, and I have been alone ever since.

ME : (AGHAST, BUT TRYING TO RESCUE THE SITUATION) Was he? Was he? Yes, yes, very distressing, yes, of course it is. I'm so sorry. Do you know, I have a feeling I actually knew that. (LAUGHING AND FOOLISHLY ATTEMPTING A JOKE) Do you know, I think I must be suffering from a case of premature Altzheimer's disease...

MRS. S.: (WITH PURSED LIPS FROM MY RIGHT) I nursed my mother for fifteen years with Altzheimer's disease. There is absolutely nothing amusing about that, I can assure you. It is a most distressing illness.

ME : (WIPING THE SMILE OFF MY FACE) Fifteen years you nursed her? Yes, yes, of course it is a distressing complaint, and no, no, of course I don't find it amusing no. Dear me (A PATHETIC ATTEMPT AT BEING ENDEAR-INGLY VULNERABLE), every time I speak I seem to put my foot in it -

MRS N. : (MOUNTING THE RESENTMENT BANDWAGON FROM DIRECTLY IN FRONT OF ME) My only uncle put his foot in an unsuspected minefield during the second world war and was killed outright. (SLIGHTLY

Continued overleaf . . .

LADIES CIRCLE MEETING REPORT
MRS. TUTTSONSON ORGANISES A 'GUT' TIME FOR ALL

Thursday the nineteenth of June at seven-thirty saw the church-hall jam-packed in parts for an address by German pastor Helga Durr. Pastor Durr, who is hoping to improve her almost non-existent English over the next few weeks, announced that the bible text for her talk was to be taken from Matthew chapter twenty-six, verse forty-one:

"THE GHOST WOULD LIKE TO BUT THE MEAT IS FLABBY."

Helga is very much enjoying a holiday with Mrs. Tuttsonson, who does bed and breakfast for fourteen pounds a night and thirteen pounds for church members, with a reduction of ten per-cent out of season, and evening meals available at varying prices if ordered in advance at time of booking. After the talk, which was applauded with puzzled enthusiasm by a selection of people from more than one part of the hall, homemade cakes, tea and coffee were supplied at very reasonable prices by Mrs. Tuttsonson, who will also be serving morning coffee, lunchtime snacks, and cream teas in her front garden during the summer months. The vicar formally thanked Mrs. Tuttsonson of Thirty-five, Willow Grove (TEL: 569342) for suggesting and arranging the evening,

Report by H. Tuttsonson.

LOCAL SAYING
Sent in by Violet Jenks

See a stoat in the morning hay,
Leave off dancing for that day.

. .Continued from previous page

TEARFULLY) I do w-wish you hadn't said that...

ME : (RATHER FAINTLY) A minefield? The second world war? Your only uncle? Yes, yes, I wish I hadn't said it too. I feel all over the place now -

MRS. N.: (INTO HER HAND-KERCHIEF) So did my uncle.

ME : (LOSING THE PLOT, AS YOUNG CURTIS WOULD PUT IT IN HIS LIVELY WAY) Yes, yes, I expect your uncle did feel like that as well, yes. Well, I don't seem to be able to get anything right, do I? Really, you know, I think it might be better if I just said nothing - nothing at all. Yes, I know, hands up all those who've been married to deaf mutes for several decades! Or perhaps I should simply leave. I can easily go - (SEEING MRS JONES DIAGONALLY OPPOSITE ME ABOUT TO SPEAK) no, Mrs. Jones, the fact that your Arthur hasn't been able to easily go for some years is of no interest to me. I know what I am. I'm just a troublesome rector. Rector, Mrs. Blenkinsop - rector! When I think of what's been thrown up from around this table - no, before anyone says anything, I'm not talking about projectile vomiting, I'm talking about folk being over-

sensitive and difficult and - (SUDDENLY REALISING THAT I MAY HAVE BECOME SOMEWHAT OVER-EXCITED) Look, I'm sorry to have sounded so very angry, especially as I feel quite sure that the fault was mine. Please, may we start all over again. Let's just forget - (SEEING MRS. S. ABOUT TO REACT AGAIN) sorry, I mean - put aside what's happened and start again. I'm sorry I blew up - (AWARE THAT MRS. N. HAS LEANED OMINOUSLY FORWARD) err... lost my temper like that. I'm rather tired and tired-ness can be a real killer can't it? (MRS. L'S TURN TO TWITCH) Sorry, I mean, err... yes, well, it's not good for Christians to be at odds -

MRS. G : (SADLY, FROM BEHIND AND TO THE RIGHT) My son has a very serious gambling problem.

ME : (A BROKEN MAN) Sorry - I'm so sorry - I really am very, very sorry....

That is a true account of events on the evening in question, and I really would greatly appreci-ate it if no more was said about the matter.

Form the disk of your vicar

Richold Hamcrout-Smedley

WASH YOUR DIRTY LINEN WITH SIMON BLEACH

Q. Dear Simon,
The extract from the bishop's talk was unintelligible. Don't you agree?

Ben

A. Dear Ben,
We-e-ell, yea and nay - know what I mean?
Simon

• • • • • • • • • • • • • • •

Q. Dear Simon,
All right, I've forgiven you for only using five words to comment on my song 'We want to have God', and I've been thinking that I probably sent you a bad example of the sort of thing I write. I now enclose one of my most recent works. I know you're going to like this one. I have only sent you the chorus, but I can send the verses as soon as you like. And I meant what I said when I first wrote - be completely honest about your reaction to this piece. As I said in my first letter, I want to follow in the footsteps of that man whose worship songs get sung all over the world. This one is called 'Gleam, Jesus gleam', and although completely original, it has just the faintest echoes of his style of writing as a sort of personal tribute.

Gleam Jesus gleam,
Stuff this place with
Jehovah's niceness,
Burn Spirit burn, and
ignite our brains.
Run torrent run,
Drench the countries
with excellentness,
Pack off your will, God,
And make it be bright.

There it is then! I'm really looking forward to your response. What should I do next?

Mike

A. Dear Mike,
Words fail me, but not, thank the Lord, half as much as they do you. You ask what should you do next. Well, candidly, I would hire an extremely capable lawyer to defend you in what promises to be the most blatant case of plagiarism in the entire history of verbal and musical piracy. Faintest echoes? Are you completely mad, man? The only original aspect of what you have done is the extraordinary degree of sheer nerve that must have been required to do it. That alone should qualify you for the Guiness Book of Records. THAT IS A JOKE! Can't you take up matchbox collecting or something? Don't send me any more things that you haven't written - or that you have written for that matter. I don't want to see them.
Simon

REPORT ON THE PARISH PICNIC IN RHYME
SATURDAY JUNE 14TH By Ephraim Jenks

The Parish Picnic, an annual event
happening once in twelve months
every year,
Was at Bate's Farm which, for
folk living not far away, was quite
conveniently near.
It didn't start too well because Mrs.
Turton sat near a wasps' nest and
got stung,
Then she ran off, and tripped face-
first into one of those pats of newly-
dropped warm, liquid dung.
Jonathan Basset, age six, got
smacked shortly afterwards for
finding this extremely funny,
George Pain, age forty, didn't,
despite laughing until his eyes
watered and his nose was runny.
Everybody came to the picnic,
except the ones who weren't there,
The idea of the meal was to have a
sort of community bring-and-share,
George Pain contributed nothing,
bcause, he said, this week he was
a bit short,
But he more than made up for that by
sharing the stuff the others brought.
After lunch the curate jumped up
and said, "Let's all have some
lively games!"
And we certainly did because
just then Mrs. Turton and her
primus went up in flames.
Someone started running around
and shouting about calling out the
fire brigade,
But Norma Clements put the whole
thing out with a nearly full bottle of
traditional lemonade.
Mrs. Turton was looking a bit sad
by now, and asked to be driven
home by her husband, Ben,
Just after the car turned out of sight
we heard a loud crash so I doubt her
troubles were quite over even then.
Things went okay after that, except
that little Ronnie Clements got ratty -
why, I'm not certain,
Unless he was upset, on a blazing hot
day, that his lemonade had been used
up on extinguishing Mrs. Turton.
Mr. Harcourt-Smedley gave a talk
about Christians not having to be
afraid at the end of the afternoon,
It was going all right until one
of the kids behind him suddenly
burst a balloon.
He'd just been saying that you only
need to be afraid if you're caught in
some serious sin,
God knows what he'd been up to,
but when he heard that noise he
jumped out of his skin.
Shortly after that people started
leaving, they'd all enjoyed it as far
as I could tell,
Especially George Pain, whose
name, most of us agree, suits him
too blinkin' well.
I've no doubt we'll have another
annual Parish Picnic in twelve
months or so,
We'll all drive up to Bate's Farm
again, although something tells me
Mrs. Turton won't go.
And I don't blame her.

POETRY CORNER
WHEN MY DAD WENT TO THE SEASIDE
By Adam Booth
(Pinched from her dad's drawer and sent in by Cissy Booth)

From Tunbridge Wells to Eridge, Heathfield, Horam, Hellingly,
Through Hailsham, Polegate, Gently Down, we saw the steam-trains fly.
Long ago, one seaside day, before the clock struck six,
As morning poured out sunshine on our pavement made of bricks,
We ran with picnic, towels and trunks, and macs, in case of rain,
To meet the bus that took us down to catch the Eastbourne train.
How smashing! How fantastic! to get off at Tunbridge Wells,
To hurry to the old West Station sniffing steam-train smells,
To board the sooty monster that would thunder down the line,
To where the screaming seagulls dived towards the froth and shine.
The journey started, soon we stopped at tiny Eridge station,
Eridge people piled inside to share our destination.
George was first to get told off - if you make nasty smells,
We're getting off at Heathfield, there's a bus to Tunbridge Wells!
Heathfield came, Heathfield went, George was smelly good,
We didn't have to go back home, we never thought we would.
Are we nearly there yet? all the children ask,
Can we have a sandwich now? I'm thirsty - where's the flask?
I hope you brought my bucket, did you bring it - are you sure?
Mum, I'm bored - I want the toilet, why can't I explore?
Is this Eastbourne? No, it's Horam. Pete's got sweets, it isn't fair,
If you saved money you'd have sweets - mum, are we nearly there?
Two men got off at Hellingly, a mystery to me,
What's the point of getting off before you reach the sea?
In and out of Hailsham, past fields of cows and sheep,
Pete was lost in comics, George was fast asleep,
But as we puffed to Polgate I could swear I smelled the sea,
And heard the crash of breaking waves as clearly as could be.
Oh, to live in Gently Down, with Eastbourne just next door,
To walk or cycle every day, in minutes, to the shore!
The engine hissed and panted, brakes were shrieking, squealing loud,
George woke, we gathered up our things and joined the Eastbourne crowd.
From Tunbridge Wells to Eridge, Heathfield, Horam, Hellingly,
Through Hailsham, Polegate, Gently Down, we saw the steam-trains fly.

SP TLIGHT 4

THE VICAR
By Henry King

I hover around the corner from the vicarage in order to arrive dead on time to do my fourth Spotlight piece. This month the subject is to be the vicar himself, the Reverend Richard Harcourt-Smedley. Interviewing the Ashbys made me feel a lot more confident, but I am a little nervous this time, especially as I have been told that the vicar tends to find unpunctual people particularly annoying. When I do knock on the front door it is opened by the vicar's secretary, Miss Fitt.

I say, "Good afternoon, I've come to interview the vicar."

Miss Fitt says, "He's already got the job. In any case, a man from the magazine is due to come round about now."

We look at each other. It is one of those moments when you ask yourself if you might possibly have slipped into some parallel universe that differs slightly from the one you usually inhabit and are used to. Finally, I hold up my notebook and biro and say, "No, I don't mean I've come to interview him for the job he's doing. I know he's got that. My name is Henry King. I am the man that the vicar is expecting, and I've come to do a Spotlight interview for The Skull - you know, the column that appears every other month in the church magazine?"

MELTING
There is a pause while this information is recorded on the hard disk of Miss Fitt's mind. Then she says, "Oh! Yes! Yes! I'm sorry! Err, would you very much mind if I were to shut the door so that you can ring the bell again and I can answer the door again so that we can start all over again and I can get it right, otherwise I shall find it very difficult to err...?"

I nod. She deletes our conversation and shuts the door before I have a chance to comment further. I ring the bell again. There is a quite unexpectedly lengthy pause, then she opens the door and says, "Yes, who is it?"

I say rather wearily, "My name is Henry King. I've come to do a Spotlight interview with the vicar."

Miss Fitt looks at her watch and says, "We were expecting you a little earlier, but do come in, the vicar is waiting for you."

I start to say something in reply but think better of it. I follow Miss Fitt through the door of the vicar's study. Miss Fitt says, "Henry King is here to see you, Reverend."

STRING
The Reverend Harcourt-Smedley looks as if, over the years, his whole physical being has been going through a gradual downward melting process. He looks up from his desk, lays down a pen, and says, "Ah, yes, of course, the interview. Miss Fitt, would you please bring some coffee and biscuits for myself and the err, the late Henry King - oh, and, perhaps in the circumstances, it would be a wise precaution for you to make a brisk tour of the vicarage in order to collect any little bits of string that may be lying around."

Another of those parallel universe moments happens, except that this time Miss Fitt and I are both staring at the vicar, wondering what on earth he can be talking about. When he realises that we are staring at him he says, "Err, merely a small, ill-judged and possibly rather out-dated attempt at humour. You may leave us, Miss Fitt. And, Mister King, please forgive my references to bits of string."

I still have no idea what he is talking about.

Miss Fitt goes out of the room and I explain to the Reverend Harcourt - Smedley that I am late because of what happened when I first knocked on the door.

PRINCIPLES

He says, "Ah, yes, Miss Fitt does indeed have a capability for thinking in a quite amazingly err - lateral manner. I realised that I was to be benefited by this sterling mental quality when, on the very first morning that she began work as my secretary, I was naive enough to ask her to take a letter, and she began to put her coat on."

Feeling a little confused, I open my notebook and read the first of my prepared questions.

"Being a vicar seems to involve being all things to all men. How do you manage to adapt to the different people that you encounter in the course of your work?"

The vicar thinks for a moment or two and then says, "I apply scriptural principles to my relationship with them, of course. Take the St. Yorick's choir, for

instance. I suppose you would not care to do that, Mister King?"

I am not sure if I should reply to this question or not. Fortunately, the Reverend Harcourt-Smedley continues.

DIVINE

"My admiration for that assemblage of persons and their devoted leader is, I am sure, exceeded by no other member of this church. They could go far, and certainly some of us sincerely hope that, in the fullness of time, they will do precisely that. Far be it from me to quibble over trivial matters of disagreement concerning their role. After all, it may be that the bible is in fact seriously misguided as to the nature of the first commandment, and that when Our Lord said 'Thou shalt love the Lord your God with all your heart and with all your soul and with all your mind', it was a divine slip of the tongue, and he actually meant to say, 'Thou shalt love, cherish, flatter, accommodate, heavily finance, prioritise and consistently defer to the church choir, particularly when that body becomes an increasingly secular one whose leader regards spiritual matters as annoying distractions from the real business of the church, which is to enhance the performance and development of the musical body that he leads.'

"As I was saying, to any small and passing resentment that I might have experienced in this context, I regularly apply a specific portion of scripture, quiet meditation on which has a most soothing effect. I refer to that passage found in the second book of Chronicles, where it is recorded that King Jehoshaphat commanded his choir to sing at the head of the army as it marched against the enemy. I cannot think of a more richly appropriate place for our own choir to occupy, and I often dwell fondly on the picture that is thus conjured up."

FISH

I am unable to work out whether all this means that the vicar likes the choir or that he doesn't, so I decide to go on to my next question, which I hope will be a simpler one.

I say, "Are you for or against renewal?"

The vicar steeples his fingers, makes his very hairy eyebrows join together in the middle, and says, "Perhaps you would be kind enough to explain to me exactly what you mean by the term 'renewal'."

I feel myself going red and I start to babble. "Well, it's when err... it's when the Holy Spirit starts to err... it's when everything that was sort of happening in the old sort of way, starts to sort of happen in the err new sort of way..." I gather myself together and try once more. "It's - well, it's when there's a feeling in a church that God is really here now, whereas before there was a feeling that he err... wasn't."

The vicar nods slowly and says, "I see. And where was he, pray, during that period when he was absenting himself from a particular church?"

I open and close my mouth like a fish.

The vicar says, "Possibly you are suggesting that God is present in some churches and not in others? If that is the case, we appear to have stumbled upon a truly startling major breakthrough in theological insight. Hitherto, unless I am greatly mistaken, it has been generally understood that God is omnipresent, but now, you, Henry King, have overturned the old order and brought us into the light of a fresh revelation that God picks and chooses between a variety of venues at the week-end, rather like a theatre-goer with a west-end season ticket, electing to be available in some, but not in others. I do hope that I have not been guilty of misconstruing your very lucid account of the nature of renew-al?"

I want to die. I say, "So, err... are you in favour of it?"

PLATE

He says, "If you are asking whether I am in favour of any member of the St. Yorick's congregation having a closer expe-rience of God than they have previously enjoyed, then my reply, rather unsurpris-ingly I should have thought, is in the affirmative."

I say, "Right! Right! Thank you very much - right!"

I lose my nerve at this point and tell the vicar that I have just remembered a pre-vious appointment and have to go. He does not seem disappointed. Just as I am walk-ing through the front door I catch a glimpse of Miss Fitt appearing with a tray bearing two cups of coffee, a plate of biscuits and a little pile of pieces of string. Why? It is a good feeling when the door closes behind me.

There can't be much wrong with the St. Yorick's ship while a man like the Reverend Harcourt-Smedley is at the helm!

SERVICES

SUNDAY

8:00 a.m. Holy Communion (snug)

9:30 a.m. Family Service

11:00 a.m. Mourning Prayer

6:30 p.m. Evening All

WEDNESDAY

10 : 30 a.m. Howdy Communion

Dave Billings here. I really do have to insist that a few people start to get their act together (no pun intended!) with regard to the Harvest Supper entertainment on the evening of September 27th. As you know I'm more than happy to organise the thing, but if no-one tells me what they intend to do, how can I be expected to do anything very constructive? Come on, folks, you can do better than this. Give me a ring or catch me at any of the morning services during the coming month. I'm going to make a point of waiting at the back with a list and a pen at both the services, and the rest is up to you. I know you can do it! Let's get the show on the road! The number's still the same -

568074.

We are hoping that lots of supporters will join us on Saturday July 19 at 2 : 00 p.m. for the cricket match that will take place on the village green between a St. Yorick's team and a team from Gently Down Pentecostal Church. The team is still one or two players short, so if you fancy you can swing a bet to good effect, contact Brian Wisney, the captain, at his dental practice in the High Street. Stumps will be drawn at 7 : 00 p.m.

LADIES CIRCLE

The Ladies Circle has asked us to remind helpers for the Fun for the Fundless day that we are meeting in the church hall at 6:00 a.m. on Saturday July 5th. I have been asked to say that all those who feel offended by the suggestion that they need to be reminded may assume that they were not intended to be the recipients of this message, and should therefore ignore it.

AN APOLOGY FROM THE EDITOR

I wish to formally apologise to Herbert Spanning for the final paragraph of my reply to his letter in last month's magazine. Unfortunately, my wife was rather tired by the time she had proof-read up to that point and she failed to notice my indication that the paragraph in question was not for publication. I wish to thank Hellbent Slapping for sparring the time to draw my attention to this mutter.

The regular **Ladies Circle** meeting for this month will take place on Thursday July 17th at seven-thirty p.m. in the Church Hall. Mrs. Glass will once again be exhibiting her perennial pants. Please feel free to come and browse through a selection that promises, as usual, to vary from the plain to the exotic. Mr. Glass will be on hand with his wife to sort out the inevitable queeries.

LYDIA

CHLOE

KATY

1st Prize
I have awarded the first prize to Lydia because her depiction of me is a remarkably acute, impressionist view of my feelings immediately after contact with certain deeply beloved, but wearing, members of the congregation.

2nd Prize
I like Chloe's representation of my face because it wears the somewhat glazed expression that I see in the mirror after P.C.C. meetings.

Equal 2nd Prize
Katy's picture must be awarded equal 2nd Prize because my dear wife Elspeth tells me that I would be completely lost without a list. In this picture there is no doubt that I have a decided list.

HOUSEHOLD HINT FLIES

Sent in by Alice Williams

Flies are easy to get rid of if you use the remedy passed on to my old granny from her old granny.

Take a rolled-up newspaper and rush around bashing them as hard as you can. Repeat if problem persists.

THE SKULL

14p

The Parish Magazine of St Yorick's, Gently Down   AUGUST

HOLIDAYS ARE AUGUST'S GOAL
UNLESS YOU'RE ME AND ON THE DOLE

FAITH IN ACTION

'Draw nigh to God, and he will draw nigh to you.'

JAMES 4 v8

VICAR : THE REVEREND RICHARD HARCOURT-SMEDLEY D.D. TEL : 569604
CURATE : THE REVEREND CURTIS WAVERLOM B.D. TEL : 563957
CHURCHWEIRDEN : MISTER C. VASEY B.A. TEL : 563749
VICAR'S SEX RECTORY : CRISPO THE FITTO C.T.A.B. TEL : 569604
SKULL CONTRIBUTIONS TO HENRY PITCHER 3, FOXGLOVE ROAD: 563328

A Letter from the Vicar

Deadly Discovered,

I have been asked on a number of occasions recently to share my views on the whole question of the modern church, and, in particular, those apparent manifestations of the Holy Spirit which characterise the type of church that one associates with the Canadian Beneficence, as I believe it is termed. Leaving aside those persons of an American bent who prophesy nationwide revival at a specific time and then feel the need to radically redefine revival when it fails to happen, let me say immediately, that, although our young people may regard me as something of an old slick-in-the-mug, I am actually in favour of anything which draws our people closer to God. My caution in these matters might best be illustrated by describing a recent encounter with an old acquaintance whom I encountered in a garage whilst waiting to pay for petrol.

I recall the occasion especially well because I had just been engaged in an infuriating discussion with my dear wife, Elspeth, who had stated that this was a particularly good place from which to procure fuel, because at this garage we were able to fill our car with thirty-six pounds worth of petrol, whereas, at a garage on the other side of the village, our tank would accommodate only thirty-four pounds worth. Elspeth and I rarely argue, but on this occasion the atmosphere that had developed between us certainly fell short of the Utopian ideal.

That is why, at first, I failed to recognise the person behind me in the queue, a man I had not seen for many years, and about whom I recalled only that he had a tendency to repeat everything that he said a number of times, a trait which is, unfortunately, highly infectious. My conversation with this person, whose name also happened to be Richard, proceeded in the following way:

ME : And how are you, Richard?
HIM : Fine, Richard, fine - fine - fine - fine - I'm fine, Richard.
ME : Oh, good - good - good - good - good - that's good...
HIM : Yeah - yeah - yeah -yeah...
ME : So, err.. do you go to church still, Richard?
HIM : Yeah, Richard, I go up Horsham - Horsham - go to Horsham - Horsham - I go up Horsham - go to Horsham...
ME : Right - right - right - right - so, err, what's it like up at err Horsham?
HIM : (SPEAKING LIKE ONE WHO HAS DISCOVERED A TASTY, CHEAPISH RED WINE) They do a very nice anointing up there, Richard, a very nice anointing.
ME : (SOMEWHAT PUZZLED) Oh! And err, what else err...

HIM : (CONVERSATIONALLY) You get flakin' out - flakin' out - you get flakin' out - you get that.

ME : (PUZZLED) Flaking out? (AS REALISATION DAWNS) Are you talking about being slain in the Spirit?

HIM : That's right, yeah, flakin' out, every Sunday, yeah, flakin' out - you get that...

ME : What else do you get?

HIM : Colin Urquhart - you get him - you get Colin Urquhart...

ME : Like a plastic soldier in a cornflake packet, you mean?

HIM : (UNCOMPREHENDINGLY) Yeah. No. Eh? Watcher mean, Richard?

We parted company shortly after that, and I was left to reflect on this strange but regrettably common view of the church as an establishment that operates as though it were a form of spiritual 'carvery'. One takes one's plate to the front, has it piled high with goodies, then returns to one's seat and gobbles it all down. I fear that my old acquaintance was simply voicing the unspoken appetites of many, and it is considerations of this kind that have placed hurdles in the path of my race towards radical change. No doubt I shall prove to be completely mistaken, but at least I shall be mistaken at my own pace.

I should add that my lively curate, Curtis, is a rather fine hurdler, and, I must reluctantly admit, a passable advertisement for the benefits of change.

From the dicks of your vicer,

Pochard Handcream-Smedley

MIRACLES EXPLAINED

(4) Turning the water into wine.

Jesus said to the servants, "Fill the jars with water," so they filled them to the brim. Then he told them, "Now draw some out and take it to the master of the banquet." They did so, and the master of the banquet tasted the water that had been turned into wine.

John 2 : 7- 9

Here we are then with the last and surely the jolliest of our short series of Miracles Explained, and in this story we see, more plainly than in any other, that our assumptions about the previous career of Jesus are totally justified. If the master had not been as closely involved with the training and performance of fish as we now know him to have been, this 'miracle' would have simply not been possible.

The whole thing becomes crystal clear when we allow one word to enter the equation. And that word is 'squid'. Yes, one of the acts in the travelling fish circus through which the master earned his pre-ministry living involved the use of a type of small squid, which must have been quite common in the Sea of Galilee in those days. This creature would have been painstakingly trained to emit its thick, inky-black liquid (a normal defence mechanism in most cephalopods) when pressure was applied to a certain part of its body. The 'turning water into wine' trick was surely likely to have been one of the most popular items in those long-ago circus presentations.

Here, at Cana, we see the master utilising his previously gained experience and skills to create a quite startling effect. Rather in the manner of a present-day magician, he must have had two or three of these little squid hidden about his person in water-filled skin containers. Using the sleight of hand that would have been part of the stock in trade of fish circus trainers, he obviously introduced one squid into each jar that had been filled with water, giving it, as he did so, the slight squeeze that constituted a command to release the aforementioned black fluid. Within seconds the water in the jars would have acquired a dark hue that, to those amazed onlookers, must have appeared to be the colour of fine wine.

What happened when the master of the banquet and others drank it? Well, as we know, they had already run out of wine, so it is reasonable to suppose that, by then, the critical faculties of all present were dulled, to say the least. Besides, the power of suggestion is very strong. It is quite amazing what people will believe if you talk absolute nonsense with sufficient confidence!

The only question that remains is - what happened to those obedient little squid? Well, it is dangerous to conjecture too far beyond the facts, of course, and I never do, but my personal view is that Jesus, a lover of all living creatures, would have carefully retrieved them from the bottoms of the jars and returned them to their hiding places beneath his robes.

For me, the real miracle of the Cana wedding was not this really quite elementary 'water-into-wine' trick, but the way in which Jesus instantly perceived a use for the skills and equipment that were available to him.

HOUSEHOLD HINT
REMOVING CAVIAR MARKS

Sent in by Lady Hilary Partington-Grey

Aren't dinner parties heavenly - I absolutely adore them. Dicky, Lucinda and Brook adore them too. We all do. But don't you simply loathe it when one of your helps finds fresh caviar stains on a favourite silk tablecloth the next day? Well, ages ago, my dear old Nanny-Blubby had a stunningly clever trick to deal with them. Tell one of your most careful ladies to mix three tablespoons each of Napolean Brandy, Cointreau, Creme de Menthe, Grande Marnier, and barely a silver thimbleful of any - yes - any liquid Chanel product. Tell her she's to dab the stain with this for literally aeons, if necessary, until the mark is completely gone. Don't forget to arrange extra wages if she has to stay past home-time.

CHAIR PLEA!

A cri de coeur from Edna Galt, who is responsible for looking after the church hall.

As the minister freely knows I am more happy than to give my unpaid voluntary services to the church in regard of looking after the hall and that, in all its regards. But how am I supposed to do my job if others do not leave the place in the manner to which it is expected that they should? They would not do it in their own homes so why not can they not do it in the hall which when all is said and done it is my job to clear up after them? Mister Pitcher and the minister have told me to come forward and express myself in front of everyone and say my piece in a piece in the church magazine so although I am not one for a lot of words or pushing myself forward I will talk about one of the things that to my mind is not right.

The thing that gets me maddest is the chairs. I have been through the chairs with the new cureit more times than I have cooked hot dinners which is a lot and he laughs and says all right but the self same thing happens every time he has one of his getting to know Jesus sessions or whatever they are called which we never used to have. Here is how the chairs are supposed to be done.

There are three different sorts of chairs and they all have to be stacked facing backwards at the back of the hall in two rows and piles of six of the same sort of chair which works out exactly right except for the newest stiff orange ones which there are two odds, which doesn't matter that they are in a pile of two because there are not four more the same to be fair.

A lot of people I talk to think the blue bendy chairs are all the same but they are surprised when I tell them that they are not. There are two lots of blue bendy chairs as I call them and both lots have got a hole in the back. This is where the misconfusion comes out. I keep finding these chairs all stacked together come what may I'm all right Jack as if it didn't matter. The thing is the holes in the backs of the oldest blue bendy chairs are a bit bigger than the holes in the backs of the ones that came just after when the minister was first induced and if you stack them with the oldest chairs they do not quite stack as straight as if you stack the oldest ones with the oldest ones or the ones that came when the minister was induced with other ones that came when the minister was induced. If you stack the oldest blue bendy chairs with the blue bendy chairs that came just after when the minister was first induced you are asking for trouble in my point of view and I will not be responsible.

When we come to the stiff orange chairs how anyone in their right minds can think they are all right to stack with any of the blue bendy ones is beyond me. Some people must be colour blind or go around with their eyes shut is all I can say. I said to my Andrew last night orange is orange and blue is blue and bendy is bendy and stiff is stiff to my mind and he said his too. Still perhaps I'm wrong. It is all right for the new cureit to say people in his getting to know Jesus palavers feel uncomfortable seeing me hovering crossly at the back as he puts it but he is not the one who has to spend half an hour afterwards sorting chairs into their

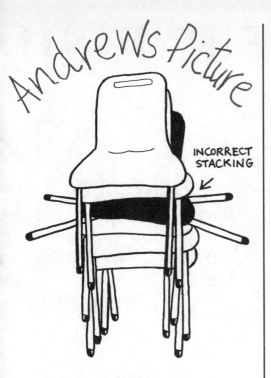

Andrews Picture

INCORRECT
STACKING

proper stacks before getting home to see to Andrew and my's little bits and pieces.

Andrew has drawn it out as to how it did not ought to be as above.

I have written all this down because last week it all came to a fruit. I come in happy as a sandcastle after my holiday to find four of the blue bendy ones that came when the minister was induced under four of the oldest ones with a stiff orange one upside down on top! Things have reached a pretty pass when you can not go away for a well earned break and trust that the chairs will be not be stacked wrong while your back is turned with one upside down. Anyway I have had my say. Who am I?

YOU ARE OLD
BISHOP STANLEY
By Victor Clements

(As many of us know, Bishop Stanley is a regular contributor to those worthy religious discussion programmes on late night television that nobody watches or understands. I have noticed that he follows every point he makes with an aggressive jutting of the chin and the words, "Don't you agree?" Victor.C.)

You are old, Bishop Stanley, your hair has turned white,
Yet, minutes ago, from this table,
You leapt through the air and you juggled in flight,
What makes you so physically able?

Well, you see, many churches insist that you sit,
But for years in the old C. of E.,
The kneeling and standing have kept me as fit,
As a teenager - don't you agree?

You are old, Bishop Stanley, but still, I am told,
Your sermons are terribly long,
Don't you think, for poor Anglicans, tired and cold,
That a two hour message is wrong?

I like to ensure, after making a point,
That its meaning is perfectly plain,
So I make it again and again and again,
And again and again and again.

You are old, Bishop Stanley, and people have said,
That you seem very pleasant and quaint,
Do you think, in the future, this being the case,
That someone will make you a saint?

If you were a C. of E. bishop, you know,
You would instantly banish the notion,
I'm not at all keen on becoming St. Stan,
I fear it would be a demotion.

You are old, Bishop Stanley, yet others would say,
As their knees were reduced to a jelly,
"I can't think of anything clever today,"
How are you so good on the telly?

I think my humility must be the thing,
I'm quite without faults, as you see,
Conceit was the last of my failings to go,
And perfection works well on T.V.

(PAUSE)

Don't you agree?

THE PARISH

**St. Yorick's
Gently Down**

versus

**Gently Down
Pentecostal
church**

Report by Lucinda
Partington-Grey

Daddy Bear - I mean Stephen - who I'm practically engaged to, asked me to come along and watch the crickety thing he was in and then write about it for the Skull thing. Mummy said I don't know a flea's willy about cricket, but I used to have real crushy-flops about Godfrey Botham and I've seen the odd trenche on telly so I said I'd have a bash. Stephen took me in one of mummy's littler cars.

I was ever so surprised by the bigness of the court. I mean - it was really gi-normous! A great big sort of distanty paddock affair with a little low rope going all round the outside that wouldn't stop a mouse getting in. I sat by the rope and wrote notes in my tiny flower-fairy notebook, and I made oodles of daisy-chains as well for

Stephen to wear with his lovely white crickety things after tea.

The referees and the crew from the other church were first to come out of the little white house where they keep the tea and pooper-pits. They sort of milled about all over the court until my Stephen and another chappie from our church came out, both holding those wooden battering things. Then everything went quiet and a man from the other church suddenly rushed crossly towards Stephen and threw a ball at him as hard as he could. He kept doing it! I literally screamed, "Look out, Daddy Bear!" every single time, to warn him. Stephen and his friend didn't do awfully well because most times they biffed the ball so hard with their battering things to make

CRICKET MATCH

sure they didn't get hit by it and hurt, that it went right over the rope at the edge of the court, and you don't seem to be allowed to run if it does that, so they can't have scored many rounders.

Both the referees were from the other church, and one of them was a complete and utter blinking cheat. Twice, when a horrid ball-thrower came literally thundering down towards Stephen, he shouted, "No ball!" Such a fib! And quite a dangerous one if my luvvy pet bear had believed him.

You could tell the other referee was from one of those funny little pentecostal churches, because three times at least, when Stephen or his friend bashed the ball right over the rope without it even touching the court, he

was so pleased that he shot his silly arms up as high as they'd go, and probably said whatever it is silly pentecostal people say under their silly pentecostal breaths.

Stephen and his friend were allowed to stay out there trying to get rounders right up to teatime, and people were really nice to them when they came back to the tea and pooper-pit place, even though they'd done so badly. They said well done for carrying their bats, which didn't seem much of a jolly achievement to me, but Stephen looked quite a pleased Daddy-Bear.

Oh - I've run out of space. I think the others must have won. They used lots more batterers.

WASH YOUR DIRTY LINEN WITH SIMON BLEACH

Q. Dear Simon,

The other day I went into a little Christian bookshop near the end of the bridge on the other side of the town. I didn't even know it existed until then. When I was talking to the two ladies who were serving behind the counter I happened to ask them what kind of church they went to.

One of them answered, "Oh, we're free evangelicals - that's what we all are here - free evangelicals".

Then they told me that they were moving to bigger premises just up the road soon, and I said, "Gosh, that'll be a big job for you."

"Yes, it will," said the other one, "but we don't lose heart because we have great faith in Mary."

What an extraordinary theological stance for free evangelicals! Do you think I've discovered a new denomination?

William

A. Dear William,

No, idiot, I know that shop, the manageress is called Mary.

Simon

. . . .

Q. Dear Simon,

I've always had a secret desire to go for a career in stand-up comedy, but I've never really felt that God was guiding me strongly in that direction. Then, the other night, I dreamed a joke! Can you imagine that? I actually dreamed a joke that I'd never heard before. I dreamed it all night - over and over again. It was amazing!

What happened in my dream was this. I found myself in charge of a fire, and I was doing very well until I ran out of wood and coal and the fire started to go out. So I turned to a woman who was standing quite nearby, and I said, "I think I'll throw my own body on the fire just to keep it burning."

And she said, "No! Don't be a fuel!"

Don't be a fuel! I dreamed it - just like that! I think the Lord was saying to me that the time has come for me to go on the boards, don't you?

Stewart

A. Dear Stewart,

No, the time has come for you to go on the <u>wards</u>, not the boards. You must have misheard him. Seriously, anyone who's capable of dreaming a joke as bad as that when he's lying down would be very ill-advised to attempt to tell any standing up, don't you think?

Simon

94

NOTICEBOARD

𝔖𝔈𝔯𝔙𝔦𝔠𝔢𝔰

𝔖𝔲𝔫𝔡𝔞𝔶

8 : 00 a.m. 𝔥𝔬𝔩𝔶 ℭ𝔬𝔫𝔫𝔢𝔠𝔱𝔦𝔬𝔫

9 : 30 a.m. 𝔉𝔦𝔩𝔢𝔶 𝔖𝔢𝔯𝔳𝔦𝔠𝔢

11 : 00 a.m. 𝔐𝔬𝔯𝔫𝔦𝔫𝔤 𝔓𝔯𝔞𝔶𝔢𝔯

6 : 30 p.m. 𝔈𝔟𝔢𝔫 𝔦𝔫 𝔓𝔯𝔞𝔶𝔢𝔯

𝔚𝔈𝔡𝔫𝔢𝔰𝔡𝔞𝔶

10 : 30 a.m. 𝔍𝔬𝔩𝔩𝔶 ℭ𝔬𝔪𝔪𝔲𝔫𝔦𝔬𝔫

Ladies Circle

Please note that the Ladies Circle will not be meeting this month as several of the ladies are away on holiday with husbands and families. However, Mrs. Tyson has sent me a little note in which she says 'I shall be at home on the morning of Thursday August 21st, and am more than willing to be taken advantage of.'

I'm sorry, but as far as I, Dave Billings am concerned, there just isn't going to be a Harvest Supper entertainment on September 27th unless somebody pulls his finger out and begins to think of something to do on the night. You'll all be coming along as usual, I have no doubt, expecting to see a show. Well, I've got news for you - there isn't going to be a show at the moment because not one single person (other than sad old you-know-who with his impression of Mussolini being hung from a lamppost) has offered me an act to put on my list. I didn't ask for this job, you know, folks, I was volunteered into it by the vicar before last. I'm not saying I mind doing it but **I've got to have a little co-operation. Please, folks! Get together! Think hard! Come up with some ideas! Stop me in the street! Come round! Ring me up! 568074 is the number. Ring it - now!**

A BIG **THANKYOU** ETHEL!

Report on the August Ladies Circle meeting by Phyllis Tyson.

The Ladies Circle meeting on July 5th was our special Fun for the Fundless day in which we annually give a warm welcome to nearly a hundred people from a deprived parish in the East End of London. Twenty-five ladies worked almost non-stop from six o'clock in the morning until gone eight o'clock before we finally cleared up the mess.

It would be nice to mention everybody by name but, of course, all of our pathetically ordinary efforts pale against the immense, humbling, wonderful, awe-inspiring coffee and cold drink preparation of Ethel Cleeve, who, despite (with more than ample justification) being deeply and desperately upset by things not going precisely to plan on at least two occasions, poured herself and her drinks out for the benefit of others in a manner which reminded those present irresistibly of the way in which the great martyrs have been burned at the stake in order that others might have life and freedom.

We cannot but bow in - yes - cringing adoration as we consider the way in which Ethel heroically endured long desert-like periods of blistering tedium while others idled away their time on food pre-paration and jolly pursuits with the visitors, and we all want to kiss her and love her and give her little presents to show that we valued her contribution above all others. All I can say to those who felt that she was unduly petty, difficult, self-centred, obstructive, consistently negative and downright bitchy on this occasion, is that they must be very small-minded and unappreciative indeed. I would like to offer sincere apologies to Ethel on their behalf and assure her that, if the right-thinking ones among us have their way, these blinkered ingrates will be drummed out of the Ladies Circle at the earliest possible opportunity.

Thank you, Ethel, once again, for contributing at least half of what turned out to be a difficult and rewarding day.

14p

THE SKULL

The Parish Magazine of St Yorick's, Gently Down   SEPTEMBER

SEPTEMBER AND THE SUMMER'S OVER
LEAVES TURN REDDER, BROWNER, MAUVER

FAITH IN ACTION

'. . . and drink of that which the young men have drawn.'

RUTH 2 v9 AV

VICAR : THE REVEREND RICHARD HARCOURT-SMEDLEY D.D. TEL : 569604
CURATE : THE REVEREND CURTIS WARVOLEM B.D. TEL : 563957
CHURCHWEIRDEN : MISTER C. VASEY B.A. TEL : 563749
VICAR'S SECRETARY : CRISPO-BABY C.T.A.B. TEL : 569604
SKULL CONTRIBUTIONS TO HENRY PITCHER 3, FOXGLOVE ROAD: 563328

A Letter from the Vicar

IF IT'S NOT ACTUALLY DEAD, WHY REVIVE IT!

Deadly Beloved,

May I warmly welcome back to the parish all those who have recently returned from their holidays.

I feel it incumbent upon me in this month's letter to refute claims made by certain members of the church that a new era of spiritual activity has been signalled by an unfortunate event that occurred at one of our morning services during the month preceding the one that will have recently concluded by the time you read this edition of The Skull. In particular, I regret the precipitate manner in which one member of this congregation, known to me, appears to have offered a somewhat excitable and highly-coloured version of the occurrance in question to one of those so-called Christian magazines which suffers, like my dear wife Elspeth's feet, from poor circulation, and resembles some desperate fugitive from the law in the sense

that it appears to find it necessary to alter its name and identity on almost every occasion that it emerges into the public domain.

As a result of the lurid article that appeared in last month's issue under the ridiculous headline YORICK BLESSING - A NEW WAVE? two coachloads of people whom I can only describe as spiritual voyeurs arrived at our communion service last Sunday to witness the phenomenon for themselves.

I did not greatly mind the fact that a considerable proportion of the congregation clapped and danced their way through 'Rock of Ages', but I did strongly object to the manner in which, during the sharing of The Peace, a succession of complete strangers with soupy, vacuous smiles on their faces embraced me as though we were long-lost relatives who had been reunited by that Cilla Black person. One young female, hippy-like person in particular, who seemed to have an inordinate number of limbs, enfolded me in a most alarming way, whispering in my ear as she did so, "The Lord wants his church back." Regrettably, I forgot myself to the extent of replying, "I know how he feels," but I was under some provocation.

I cannot help feeling that our visitors must have been disappointed with the service itself, except for one moment during the recently inserted "praise" section, when a number of them clearly believed that Henry Plumpton had begun to sing in tongues, not realising that the rendition of "Majesty" by a man with no roof to his mouth produces a markedly similar effect.

The incident which gave rise to this misguided talk of a "Yorick Blessing" can be very simply explained, and is due almost entirely to the introduction by Curtis, our new curate, who is blessedly lively, and, if I may say so, resembles the egg that is traditionally offered to members of his race, of that same "praise" session to which I have already alluded. In the entire period before Curtis arrived to lead us into the modern age, or "B.C.", as I increasingly tend to think of it nowadays, the congregation were in no doubt whatsoever about correct conduct during the singing of a hymn. They stood. They did not sit. They rumbled and shuffled themselves into corporate erectness after one line of the hymn had been played. Those who did sit were those who had to sit because they could not stand. It was very simple.

On the Sunday in question, the problem was exacerbated by the fact that the front pew on one side of the church was exclusively (and some-what perversely, since they invariably station themselves at the back of the church) occupied by an extremely large contingent of the Diblings, that dear family whose members are uniformly hard of hearing.

(I ought to add, incidentally, that,

Continued overleaf . . . .

PRAYERS FOR THE MONTH
Sent in from all over the parish

For Vince, nervous near photo-copiers after years of bullying... For Avril, still unframed... For Dennis, that the angle might increase daily... For Dilly and Craig, so disappointed, that a far, far better theodolite will come... For Penelope, always a club short... For Vernon, unlucky with fertiliser... For Jerome, a respected friend and adored postman, that his desire may be within reach... For Sylvia, that the tissues will burn easily, and that the plumber might then willingly return... For Glen, that steam may not be the only product of his boiling... For Anthony, in despair over the loss of his friend, that the opportunity for a speech might arise... For Lester, that he will put himself first for once... For Jeremy, that he might master the desired rhythm and adjust his output... For Abigail, that inflation will not have the effect she fears... For Pedro, special person, that he will agree to change his name.. For Ruth, that she might turn from cylindrical sculpture and be close to her badger once more... For Isaac, unable to forgive himself, that he may remember what he did...

Amen.

LOCAL SAYING
Sent in by Ephraim Jenks

Full moon at night, moonlight.

Continued from previous page

after the event I am about to describe, Curtis finally managed to persuade me to agree that, in order to cater for those afflicted in such a way, I should have what I believe is known as a "coil" fitted as soon as possible to avoid unwanted distur- bances in the future.)

The Diblings failed to appre- hend an instruction, or should I say a warmly encouraging suggestion, from Curtis (Curtis does not believe that we should "instruct" the flock) that everyone should remain seated during the first item in the "praise" session. The entire row of Diblings rose to their feet after the music commenced, only to descend once more on registering the fact that the rest of the congregation had remained seated. The occupants of the second row, seeing the front row stand and assuming that they must have misunderstood what Curtis had said, rose to their feet, but sat down again almost instantly on observing that the Diblings had changed their minds. The third row slavishly followed the example of the second row, to be succeeded by the immediate rise and fall of the fourth row, who were copied by the fifth row, and the sixth, and the seventh, and the eighth, and the ninth and so on to the back of the church.

It was at this point that the writer of the aforesaid article, who was sitting on the other side of the church, raised his hand in that manner particularly suggestive of an infant desperately in need of the toilet, and shouted, "Yes! The blessing has come! Hallelujah!"

In fact, the blessing has not come, and if the blessing, whatever the blessing is, does come, I consider it unlikely in the extreme that it will appear in the form of a purely accidental Mexican Wave, as I believe such patterns of movement are termed at sporting events.

On a separate subject, I have given much serious consideration to the request put to me by Curtis and a small group of people who generally sit at the back, that we should institute regular healing services into the pattern of our worship. The wardens and I can see no real harm in such an institution, and I therefore propose that in every alternate month which has five Sundays in it, the evening service on that fifth Sunday should be used as a healing service, to be arranged and led by Curtis, whose liveliness is most pungently manifested in such areas. The next but one month containing a fifth Sunday will be March of next year, and therefore the first of these meetings will take place on the 29th of that month. The next twelve months will be regarded as a trial period. If healings take place we shall, of course, continue with the practice.

From the desk of your vicar,

Riphard Hancock-Swedely

100

WASH YOUR DIRTY LINEN WITH SIMON BLEACH

Q. Dear Simon Bleach,

I trust that the outrageous 'Miracles Explained' series has now come to an end. I cannot remember ever reading such a load of unfounded, half-baked, sacrilegious piffle in my entire life. Who does this man think he is, coming out with such rubbish? Fish circus - I ask you!! This sort of thing could have a very damaging effect, especially on children and simple believers, and should never have been allowed to appear in the first place. In my view the editor deserves to be heavily censured, and if I ever meet the writer of this nonsense I shall certainly give him a piece of my mind!

Victor Clements

A. Dear Victor,

First, as the anonymous writer of the series you mention (well, I did go to Durham once), I feel rather flattered that it has provoked such a strong reaction in you, and in other readers who have spoken and written to me. Secondly, as someone who believes totally in the miracles of Jesus, I am glad that the absurdity of the general thesis was not lost on you. I hope it will inspire all of us to (a) resist such nonsense wherever we come across it, and (b) rejoice in the certainty of what we know to be true. As for you giving me a piece of your mind, Victor - well, we all know the value of the widow's mite, but I think you're going to need all you've got. Cheers!

Simon.

● ● ● ● ● ● ● ● ● ● ● ● ● ●

Q. Dear Simon Bleach,

Last month you called someone 'idiot' because he had made a quite understandable mistake. I just want to say that, as Christians, we are not allowed to call our brothers names like that.

Philip

A. Dear Philip,

Do you honestly think I don't know that? Dumbo!

Simon.

● ● ● ● ● ● ● ● ● ● ● ● ● ●

Q. Dear Simon,

I fell and cracked a bone just as I was boarding a Virgin flight at Gatwick. Is this what they call an airline fracture?

An anonymous traveller

A. Dear Anonymous traveller,

Don't waste my time, George Pain, and don't be silly. You have never been on any plane, ever, in your whole sad life. Or was your silly little verse for August a bit of a porky-pie?

Simon

● ● ● ● ● ● ● ●

NOTE FROM THE EDITOR

We have received a number of letters from readers of last month's Skull, expressing puzzlement about the exact meaning of Helga Durr's prayer. After studying it carefully myself, and speaking to Helga, I am now able to offer the complete translation:

"Lord, we hold up our hands to you, praising your mighty works, and we seek your will in our daily walk with you. **Amen."**

Incidentally, Helga, who has now returned to Germany, asked me to pass on the following message to all the friends she has made here in Gently Down:

"God rate, and may we flesh once more in the capacity of a common herb."

I think I've worked it out - small prize to the first reader who sends me the solution!

POETRY CORNER
NURSERY

Jack and Jill went up the hill,
To fetch a pail of water,
Jack fell down and broke his crown,
But that doesn't mean there isn't a God.

Jack and Jill went up the hill,
To fetch a pail of water,
Jack fell down,
And had an amazing experience of the Holy Spirit.

Wee Willie Winkie runs through the town,
Upstairs and downstairs in his nightgown.
If this kind of conduct doesn't shortly change,
We'll have to book him in to spend a week at Ellel Grange.

Little Bo-peep has lost her sheep,
And feels too untutored to find them,
Never mind college, she needs Word of Knowledge,
To name them, and claim them and bind them.

RHYMES!

ADAPTED FOR THE CHURCH

By George Pain

Little Miss Muffet sat on a tuffet,
Eating her curds and whey,
Down came a spider and sat down beside her,
So she said, "I rebuke you, and I take dominion over you,
and I tell you to go - right now!
But it didn't, so Miss Muffet was frightened away.

Hickory, dickory dock,
Two mice ran up the clock,
The clock struck one,
Missed the other one,
Because, friends, it was an anointed, spirit-filled mouse.

Humpty Dumpty had a bad winter,
Spring wasn't pleasant at all,
The summer was dreadful,
But then, at the end of August, he stopped
sitting on the wall at last, and invited the
Lord Jesus Christ into his heart, and that's why -
Humpty Dumpty had a great fall.

COLIN VASEY
By Henry King

I walk round the corner from my house to Willow Grove to interview Colin Vasey, one of our churchwardens, for this month's Spotlight. Colin lives on his own in a single-storey bungalow four or five doors down from Mrs. Tuttsonson's Bed and Breakfast establishment. When she hears that I am coming to Willow Grove she asks me to mention that she offers special reductions to church members and their friends or relations. Well - there. I have, haven't I?

Colin is tall and thin and unblinking with badly-cut short hair and a concave face shaped like a tilted crescent moon with knobbly ends. When he lets me in he is wearing a suit and tie. I have never seen Colin wear anything except a suit and tie, even to the beach and the church picnic. Colin has never been married or engaged even though he is more than forty years old. I don't mean anything in particular by that.

BLACKCURRANT

We sit in his brown sitting-room where there are no pictures on the walls, drinking glasses of blackcurrant juice squeezed out of unused individual cardboard cartons bought in advance for daily use by Colin when he went away on a coach holiday earlier in the year. I notice that two or three shelves of his bookcase are filled with what look like complete sets of Star Trek and Doctor Who books and videos.

I ask Colin what he, as a churchwarden at St. Yorick's, believes about God.

He says, "I definitely think there is something. What I mean is, I think there is something else out there that is definitely greater than us."

I say, "Oh. What sort of a something?"

He says, "Well, maybe a sort of cloud of knowingness or completeness. I definitely feel sometimes that I'm part of a complicated system of creative forces that is contained within an otherness that relates to us on a deep level."

SWARMS

And I sometimes wonder about electricity - whether there could be something like a huge, cerebral, brain-like complex that encircles all, and is fuelled by power from the worldwide socket system."

I suggest that this view might be seen as moving just a tad away from the orthodox Christian position, and I ask Colin what he considers to be the role of the church.

He says, "Okay, I think church is a central, sort of hub thing, where all the swirling atom swarms are linked into straight lines of molecular orderliness, and the people are drawn into cosmically designed patterns by the power of that linking."

We sit in silence for a few

seconds. I nod slowly and seriously, but feel severely handicapped by the fact that I have not the faintest idea what he is talking about. Eventually, I say, "What has been your most profound spiritual experience?"

Colin says, "I remember once walking through a very large field at night by accident - "

I say, "By accident?"

He says, "Yes, by accident, and I had this awareness of a sort of bright, glowing presence that was not so much visible as emanating from the edge of consciousness, as though it was being radiated down through the stratosphere straight into the minds of receptive humans like myself. That was very special - probably the really key experience of my life."

SUBCONSCIOUS

There is another thoughtful silence. I say, "Right, so, err... what about the future?"

He says, "My view is that when those circle things in the cornfields have been properly explained our whole perception of potential relationships with galactic entities will alter and we won't have to speak or pray or anything any more, because we'll be caught up into the unity of universal spirituality."

I say, as though some deep truth has at last been revealed to me, "Aaaah, yes - yes, I see what you're saying." This is not true.

I cannot think of anything else to ask, so I point towards his Star Trek and Doctor Who books in the bookcases and laugh and say, "Well, you're certainly not short of fiction, Colin, are you?"

He does not laugh at all. He shakes his head and says, "Actually, fiction isn't quite the word I would want to use about the contents of those - well, I prefer to call them journals. I believe there is an ongoing parallelness between the events in those books and the subconscious journey patterns that inhabit the ethos of our daily existence."

I say, "Oh, really, how fascinating! I had absolutely no idea...."

SUGAR

Colin asks if I would like him to make us some coffee, and explains that, although he never uses sweetening agents because such substances are almost certainly anti-lifeforce, he does have some sachets of sugar tucked away in his bedroom somewhere that he collected during his last coach holiday but two. I decline his offer, and ask a final question. Does he consider there to be any conflict between the beliefs that he has just told me about and his position as a churchwarden at St. Yorick's?

He looks very slightly panic-stricken and says, "Oh, no, I've always been Church of England - that's all right. I really like the vicar and I enjoy being a churchwarden."

As the front door closes behind me a few minutes later I reflect on the fact that the Starship St. Yorick's is unlikely to go off course while it is safely in the hands of men like Lieutenant Colin Vasey.

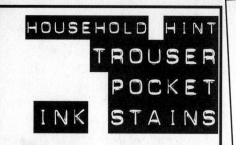

HOUSEHOLD HINT
TROUSER
POCKET
INK STAINS

Sent in by Jane Basset

Does your man persist in leaving leaky old pens in trouser pockets? Here's an answer to hard-to-shift pocket ink-stains. First, fill a big basin with crushed peanuts, Piccalilli sauce, and talcum powder. Blend to a stiff, gritty paste. After making your man put on his inky trousers, tell him to simply plunge his hand (both hands if two of his pockets are affected) into the substance. When his hands are coated with the mixture he must shove them deep into his pockets, then set off to walk for sixty minutes, during which those hands must not be removed from his pockets. On his return, all trace of the ink-stains will be gone.

While my non-Christian flatmate has been away I have collected together over a hundred of his cassette tapes of secular music, painstakingly but illicitly copied over the last ten years. I would like to swop them for a similar sized collection of spiritual music to present him with as a surprise on his return. This could be the turning point in his life. If you have a vision of my flatmate's face when he sees that he now owns over a hundred Christian tapes in place of his worldly collection, **do ring 639724.**

This is Dave Billings and it's judgement time. Not one single person has contacted me about the Harvest Supper Entertainment on September 27th, and all the obvious candidates that I've actually asked have come up with feeble excuses. I shall now take a leaf out of the book of he who provides an example for us all. You may recall the parable of the Wedding Feast, in which the formally invited guests came up with similar excuses for not coming and were rejected in the end. The bridegroom then went out into the highways and byways and invited anyone and everyone who wanted to come. And that's precisely what I intend to do now. I don't want your sophisticated acts any more, thank you very much, and when you see what the final performance consists of I hope you'll be satisfied. **Someone else can do it next year.**

This year's third meeting of the P.C.C. will take place on Thursday September 11th at 7:30 p.m. in the vicarage. Please consider attending if you happen to be a member and have ever found yourself idly wondering what happens at such events.

NOTICEBOARD

𝕾𝖊𝖗𝖛𝖎𝖈𝖊𝖘

𝕾𝖚𝖓𝖉𝖆𝖞
8 : 00 a.m. 𝕳𝖔𝖑𝖞 𝕮𝖔𝖒𝖒𝖚𝖓𝖎𝖔𝖓
9 : 30 a.m. 𝕱𝖑𝖆𝖎𝖒𝖞 𝕾𝖊𝖗𝖎𝖔𝖚𝖘
11 : 00 a.m. 𝕸𝖔𝖗𝖓𝖎𝖓𝖌 𝕻𝖗𝖆𝖞𝖊𝖗
6 : 30 p.m. 𝕰𝖛𝖊𝖓𝖎𝖓𝖌 𝕻𝖗𝖆𝖞𝖊𝖗

𝖂𝕰𝕯𝕹𝕰𝕾𝕯𝕬𝖞
10 : 30 a.m. 𝕳𝖎𝖑𝖑𝖞 𝕮𝖔𝖒𝖒𝖎𝖓𝖌𝖑𝖎𝖓𝖌

Don't forget that the Harvest Supper is happening anyway, folks, even if the entertainment turns out to be a little below par. Collect your tickets at the door round about half-past six on the 27th. The food is likely to be goo, and a bad show featuring acts from the highways and byways promises to be more entertaining than a quite good one. Am I wrong?

All members of the Ladies Circle who feel strongly about the departure of Ethel Cleeve are warmly invited to participate in a lynch-party picnic at twelve-thirty on Thursday September 11th underneath the old oak tree by the village pond, where Eileen leaving us will be high on the agenda

The Mother and Toddler Group

will resume their weekly sessions on **Friday the 12th of September from 2:00 p.m. to 3:15 p.m.** Mrs Turnbury will be in charge as Gloria is busy with a short intensive curse on working with mothers and children.

After a succession of reported disagreements between groups using the church hall it has been decided to call an emergency meeting of all hall-users on Wednesday September 24th at 7 : 00 p.m. in the church hall itself, to be chaired by the vicar. If you feel that you should be there and have not yet been asked, please ring the vicar's secretary on 569604. Come and hate your say.

Our first Guide meeting after the summer break will be on Tuesday September 9th at 7 : 00 p.m. in the church hall. We shall be planning a link-up with the Mother and Toddler group one Friday afternoon soon, when we hope that guides will offer to walk the toddlers out to the church flowerbeds to do some weeing.

I'm happy to announce that the Children's Corner will be taken over for the next three months by Russell Bleach, and will actually be a Children's Page, as you can see from this first instalment of **'Jesus and Zak'**.

THE SKULL

14p

The Parish Magazine of St Yorick's, Gently Down   OCTOBER

IN OCTOBER WE REMEMBER
THINGS THAT HAPPENED IN SEPTEMBER

FAITH IN ACTION

'Simon Peter went up and drew the net . . .'

JOHN 21 v 11AV

VICAR : THE REVEREND RICHARD HARCOURT-SMEDLEY D.D. TEL : 569604
CURATE : THE REVEREND CURTIS WARVMOLE B.D. TEL : 563957
CHURCHWEIRDEN : MISTER C. VASEY B.A. TEL : 563749
VICAR'S SECRETARY : CRISPO-BABY C.T.A.B. TEL : 569604
SKULL CONTRIBUTIONS TO HENRY PITCHER 3, FOXGLOVE ROAD : 563328

A Letter from the Vicar

Deafly Begloved,

Last month will have seen many of our dear youth experiencing new things in their lives as they moved classes or schools or took that major step which is part of growing up for all young people, namely, moving from education into the big wide world of unemployment. Some, of course, have taken the much lager step to university. But then, the Christian walk involves many changes for all of us, does it not? I, myself, for instance, felt a strong prejudice against the ordination of women for many years. Nowadays, however, my eyes have been opened and I can see that fiddling and fussing with make-up when a service is due to start, disappearing every five minutes to have babies, and being impossible to live with for at least a week in every month,

is far from being the whole story. Apart from anything else I think it likely that a female priest would add a welcome domestic dimension to cerebral, academic and spiritual layers of the ministry.

I thought it might be helpful this month, as, perhaps, some of us are seeking to change our view of God, to look at the word 'CHANGES' as a mnemonic, that is, a simple memory aid, in which each letter begins a relevant word. So, let us proceed:

C is for **COLOSTOMY BAG**, and certainly some of us are needing to go in a different direction, aren't we? And why not?

H is for **HORMONES**. Some of us have got more hormones than others, haven't we? Some of us are quite **HAIRY**, aren't we? There's another word beginning with H. I wonder, if it were possible, would we be willing to share our hormones or our hair? I do **HOPE** so - oh, look, there's another, smaller word beginning with H.

A is for **ABERDEEN**. Some of us have been to Aberdeen, haven't we? Most of us came back as soon as possible, didn't we?

N is for **NORMAN WISDOM**. I really only wanted the word "wisdom", but I had to have the Norman bit in order to have the wisdom. So, on this occasion, let's show how flexible the church is capable of being by calling it **NISDOM**. We all need lots of **NISDOM**.

    G is for **GRAHAM TAYLOR**. Some of us fear that we are failures, don't we? But let's take a lesson from Graham Taylor himself. Having failed as manager of England, he didn't give up, did he? No, he pulled himself together and went on to fail as manager of Wolverhampton Wanderers.

    E is for **EMBLEMATIC RECONSTITUTION OF ARTERIALLY DIVERSIFIED DISPENSATIONALISM**, and I think that speaks for itself, doesn't it?

    Finally, **S** is for **SALISBURY PLAIN**. Some of us feel a little bit flat sometimes, don't we? Well, all I can say to you is - let the army run all over you. I do.

    So, dear frieds, there we have it. **COLOSTOMY BAGS, HOR-MONES, ABERDEEN, NIS-DOM, GRAHAM TAYLOR, EMBLEMATIC RECONSTITUTION OF ARTERIALLY DIVERSIFIED DISPENSATIONALISM** and **SALISBURY PLAIN**. A simple little memory aid, and if all that doesn't change us, I shall be very, very surprised.

From the deck of your vicar

Richand Hardcourt-Smedley

PRAYER FOR THE MONTH
By Glenda Andrews

Our prayers are humbly offered up for Eileen Grable, spinster of this parish, particularly beseeching thee that her recent and quite frequent visits to 35 Larchwood Avenue should not be regarded as an indication that she is in any way involved in immoral behaviour with George Moat, recently widowed and resident at that address.

    Lord, vouchsafe that it may become clear to those neighbours who have observed that she sometimes fails to leave until the early morning that there could be any number of excellent reasons for such apparently suggestive behaviour on the part of thine servants.

    And stop thou the mouths, oh, Lord, we pray, of those who, having seen her buying far more eggs, bacon, cornflakes and marmalade at the Eight-Till-Late than she could possibly need for herself, find it necessary to wantonly spread cruel and unsubstantiated rumours about the relationship of these two lonely people who have almost certainly learned to find innocent, simple pleasure in each other's company - all night.

    Amen.

LOCAL SAYING
Sent in by Ashley Parr
Chewing moss that's soaked in beer
Will bring true love within the year

MORE ... NURSERY

Ding, dong bell,
Pussy's in the well.
Who put her in?
The reverend Tommy Green,
Who pulled her out?
The reverend Tommy Snout.
Bound to be a schism,
Over feline baptism.

Jack Sprat would eat no fat,
Because he had a crush on Rosemary Conley.

Hey, diddle-diddle, the cat and the fiddle,
The cow jumps over the moon,
The little dog laughs to see such fun,
And the dish runs away with the spoon.
Such things happen frequently,
On Sunday nights at H.T.B.

There was an old lady who lived in a shoe,
She had so many children she didn't know what to do,
Except in one department, obviously.
The ministry team are going round next Tuesday.

RHYMES!

ADAPTED FOR THE CHURCH
By George Pain

Mary, Mary, quite contrary,
How does your garden grow?
With silver bells and cockle shells,
And other New Age trinkets.
It's the thin edge of the occult wedge, Mary, love, isn't it?

Incey-wincey spider climbed
the water spout,
Gave up on God when the rain
flushed him out.
Out came the sun, dried up all
the rain,
Incey-wincey spider found his
faith again.

Twinkle, twinkle, little star,
Bringing wise men from afar,
You owe God an apology,
For dabbling in astrology.

REPORT ON HALL-USERS MEETING
Condensed minutes taken by Miss C. Fitt

THOSE PRESENT:
The Reverend Richard Harcourt-Smedley - Chairman
Graham Clark - Youth Club
Gloria Dowson - Mothers and Toddlers
Reverend Curtis Woverlam - Getting to know Jesus group
Sally Cumbersome - Guides
Phyllis Tyson - Ladies Circle
Edna Galt - Caretaker
Christine Fitt - Sometimes goes in and dances on her own to ballet music on a tape.

The vicar called the meeting to order.

Gloria Dowson said it was a pity it wasn't the youth club that was being called to order.

Graham Clark said it was a pity frustrated old biddies couldn't find something better to do than constantly criticise others.

Phyllis Tyson said that she thought Graham Clark was very rude and shouldn't be in charge of young people if he was going to talk like that.

Sally Cumbersome said she wanted to talk about mugs.

Edna Galt said she wanted to talk about chairs.

Graham Clark said he wanted to talk about poo and paint.

The vicar said "Ladies! Ladies!"

Graham Clark said that, as a point of order, he was a man.

Gloria Dowson laughed in a loud, sarcastic sort of way.

Graham Clark got up and said he wasn't staying to be insulted.

The vicar shouted very loudly and went bright red in the face.

Graham Clark sat down again.

The vicar asked everybody to take a deep breath and relax and look at the agenda rather than calling out all the time.

Phyllis Tyson said she hadn't been sent an agenda, and that although the Ladies Circle didn't use the hall all that much she did think that she should have been sent an agenda like everybody else.

Graham Clark suddenly found a scrap of paint on his chair and wanted everybody to come and look at it.

Everyone except the vicar and the curate crowded round to look at the paint.

Gloria Dowson said that it wouldn't surprise her if Graham Clark had put it there himself.

Graham Clark said that if Gloria Dowson was in India she'd be sacred.

Everybody started shouting at everybody else.

The curate fell off his chair and lay clutching his chest and groaning.

Everyone stopped shouting and got very worried about the curate.

The curate suddenly sat up and said he'd only pretended to be taken ill because he couldn't stand hearing all these nice people arguing with each other when we were supposed to be followers of Jesus who loved one another.

All the others sat back down again and looked a bit ashamed.

The curate suggested that he should say a prayer before we carried on with the meeting.

Phyllis Tyson cried and started talking about something that I wasn't allowed to put in the minutes.

The vicar said we'd just talk to each other for a while and fix another time for a meeting.

I was told to stop making notes, except that we had coffee after that and it was quite nice.

WASH YOUR DIRTY LINEN WITH SIMON BLEACH

Q. Dear Simon,

Please help me.

A couple of weeks ago I left home for work and realised as I was walking along the pavement that I had left my briefcase behind. There were several people on both sides of the road, and I thought it would look a little foolish if I just turned abruptly round and began to walk in the opposite direction, so, before turning back, I made loud clicking noises with my tongue and sort of sighed and snapped my fingers in an annoyed way, as one does, to show that I'd suddenly remembered having left something behind.

Later that evening I found myself reflecting on the fact that Christians shouldn't need to go though such ridiculous pantomimes just to avoid looking silly. Who cares what people think? That's what I said to myself. I resolved that the very next time I left something behind I would simply turn round and go back without any silly play-acting.

My chance came a few days later, when I realised, minutes after leaving home, that I had left my railway season-ticket behind. Bearing in mind my decision, I did not miss a stride, but wheeled round and headed briskly in the opposite direction without any display of emotion at all. I had taken only a very few steps when I recalled that my ticket was in the side pocket of my briefcase which I always take to work. Again I unhesitatingly turned straight round and set off towards the station. After approximately the same number of strides I became aware that I had forgotten my briefcase. True to my earlier decision I did an immediate about-turn and started for home yet again. It was after another five strides or so that I remembered today was a training day, and that as I would not be needing my briefcase I had put my ticket in the inside pocket of my jacket last night. Turning to resume my journey to the station I covered only the same amount of ground as I had done previously before registering the fact that I was not wearing the same jacket as I had worn the day before.

It was just after I had turned and was about to cover the same few yards of pavement for the sixth time, that I realised a small crowd had gathered on the other side of the road, and seemed to be finding me an object of peculiar interest. Of course, from their point of view it might have appeared rather odd that a man should pace fiercely up and down the same fifteen feet of a public path six times for no apparent reason, but had they been privy to the thought processes that I have explained in detail to you, they would, of course, have understood how sane and rational my actions actually were.

Anyway, my question is this. Bearing in mind what happened on the above occasion, should I try a different approach? This is my idea. Next time I am walking along the pavement and I realise that I have left something behind I shall stop, attract the attention of the other people in the street by waving vigorously, and call out something like this:

"Right, everybody! Gather round, please - this'll only take a moment or so. Right, well, I've just got you all together to say that I'm on my way to work and I've suddenly remembered that I've left something behind, so in a moment you'll see me turn round, without any of this silly signalling business, and start walking back to get it. May look a bit loony, but in fact it's not at all, just an ordinary piece of forgetfulness dealt with in an entirely sensible and normal manner. Well, that's it - please feel free to carry on now. Thank you for taking the trouble to assemble and listen and I hope you all have a very good day."

Do you think this will simplify matters?

Vaughn

A. Dear Vaughn,

I suggest that you concentrate more on curing your forgetfulness than working out how to cope with changing direction in public, otherwise matters may be simplified to the extent that you find yourself in a situation where you have only fifteen feet to negotiate, whichever direction you go in, with nice soft walls to protect your head if you try to go any further.

Simon

● ● ● ● ● ● ● ● ● ● ● ● ● ● ●

Q. Dear Simon Bleach,

I have no doubt that my two previous complaints about George Pain's ludicrous verses at the head of each magazine were extremely tedious in your eyes, and I have done my best to swallow my reactions to his monumentally ridiculous offerings from April to August, but I really cannot contain myself when it comes to September's issue. Autumn is, for me, a season of almost sacred beauty. I deplore its trivialisation by Pain, who, merely in order to effect a cheap rhyme with 'over', describes autumn leaves as becoming 'mauver'. Leaves do not turn mauve, and therefore they do not turn mauver! They do not! They do not! They do not! They turn yellow and red and gold and brown. They do not turn mauve! They do not!

Hilda

A. Dear Hilda,

Thank goodness there are still a few folk like you who are willing to stand up and be counted over major conflicts like this. It is incredible to think, is it not, that some people, probably fiddling around foolishly with third-world issues, are not even aware of the mauve leaf issue?

Simon

● ● ● ● ● ● ● ● ● ● ● ● ● ● ●

Q. Dear Simon,

Two months ago, while I was waiting for the doctor to come and deal with my airline fracture, I asked a man who lives on the edge of the airport if property was expensive in his area. He told me houses were cheap because of the low overheads.

George the not anonymous any more traveller

A. Dear George,

One more joke and I tell everyone your secret.

Simon

● ● ● ● ● ● ● ● ● ● ● ● ● ● ●

Q. Dear Simon,

I am very depressed at present because, although I write long, spiritually sustaining pastoral letters to all sorts of people all the time, no-one ever replies. This is such a chronic problem that I am seriously beginning to think that there may be some spirit of demonic restraint at work. In a sense this is encouraging and exciting because it shows that I must be doing something

right, doesn't it? But how do I combat the force of evil that is corrupting the work I do?

A. Dear whatever your name is and wherever you are,

I suppose it is remotely possible that a spirit of demonic restraint is at work, but, after much thought and prayer, I personally lean towards the slightly more prosaic theory that failure to add your name and address when you write letters might be a much more significant factor in this area.

(Like this) Simon

P.S. *You should be aware that the addition of your name and address to these spiritually sustaining letters is still no guarantee that they will be answered - absolutely nothing to do with demons, you understand.*

● ● ● ● ● ● ● ● ● ● ● ● ● ● ●

Q. Dear Bleach,

As organist and choirmaster at St. Yorick's, I become very annoyed by reports I hear of negative talk about myself and about the musical aspects of this church.

To demonstrate that we musicians are not as narrow, obsessive, dull and humourless as some people seem to think, I would like the readers of this magazine to see the following extract from a letter, sent by me to my son, also a musician, currently studying for a music degree at university, in response to a letter stating his concern that he had so far been unable to find rented accomodation for his second year, and asking if I knew anyone in the area who might be able to help. I wished to say to him that I foresaw no great difficulties ultimately, and that as long as he presented himself without affectation, viewed at least six or seven options before making up his mind, and exercised his full faculties in the selection process, he would undoubtedly find something suitable eventually. In order to entertain him I couched part of my message in the following terms:

This **Note** is to say that, although I can pull no **Strings**, there is little need to **Fret**. I do not **C Major** problems in securing the **Key of A Flat**. **Stave** off worry, **Treble** your efforts and do not **Quaver**. Simply **B Natural**, **C Fifth**, **C Sixth**, **C Seventh**, and **B Sharp**, as you have been since you were **A Minor**.

Is that dull? I don't think so. It all makes me so angry!
Herbert Spanning.

A. Dear Spanning,
*If you don't stop getting so **Crotchety**, I bet you a **Tenor** you'll end up having a **Harp-attack**. See? I'm not dull either!*
Bleach

HOUSEHOLD HINT
STAINS

Sent in by Lily (I'M 83!) Forrest

Dealing with unsightly stains left by tea or coffee cups on wooden surfaces need not be a problem. Add two drops of Hydrochloric acid to one tablespoon of lemon curd, and rub hard into stain with the skin of a freshly flayed mole.
Leave overnight and wash off in the morning with a sponge soaked in cold tea.

Vacancy available in two-person flat owing to previous occupant's abrupt departure and temporary hospitalisation. Applicants may be Christians if they wish, but must have no views whatsoever on the recording of music. **Ring 639724**

NOTICEBOARD

SERVICES
SUNDAY
8:00 a.m. Holy Communion

9:30 a.m. Family Nervous

11:00 a.m. More or less Prayer

6:30 p.m. Evening Player
WEDNESDAY
10:30 a.m. Goaly Communion

This month's Ladies Circle meeting will be held on Thursday October 13th in the church hall, where Mrs. Veegley of Meopham will address us on the subject of 'The Danglers of Dribbling in the Occult'. Mrs. Veegley is the wife of Jerome Veegley, the art critic, whose best-known book is 'The Sphere in Contemporary Art'. Before her conversion she was, herself, a watch.

Why should the devil have all the best parties, eh?

On Friday October 31st non-Christian young people will be dressing up in bizarre costumes and going from door to door in the dark, offering householders the choice of giving them sweets, food and money, or having some diabolical trick played on them. Then they'll probably go on to some wild party where there's loud music and dancing and strong drink and lots of other young people all celebrating Halloween until the early hours of the morning. But we don't want all that, do we, young Christian people? Because from 7:00 a.m. until 10:30 p.m. we're going to follow them around doing door to door evangelism before going back to have a party of our own in the church hall, and it's going to be a Not-Halloween Party! How about that? We'll have more fun than them, won't we? We'll have table-tennis, and squash and sausages on sticks and a Spring Harvest Tape coming over the speaker. Hope to see lots of you there.

PUBLIC ANNOUNCEMENT

Fungil and Foskitt Undertakers wish to announce, with regret, that they are unable to accept commissions for the first fortnight of October due to the number of clients requiring their services. May we also take this opportunity to publicly request that, during periods such as this, people should desist from the practice of telephoning the firm to ask if anybody has 'dropped out'.

REPORT ON HARVEST FESTIVAL ENTERTAINMENT
SEPTEMBER 27TH By Dave Billings

I am, of course, grateful to all those who did take part in the Harvest Festival entertainment, and I am sure I will, in time, freely forgive those who said they would be taking part but never actually got round to letting me know what exactly they were going to do, but I think it is worth reflecting on the fact that this year's entertainment might have been just a tad livelier if there had been a somewhat wider selection of acts to choose from. Nor did I greatly appreciate some of the ribald comments issuing from the back of the hall, particularly as these comments appeared to emanate chiefly from those very individuals who had assured me that they would make a special effort to "do something really good this year". Here is my account of the extraordinary programme that was offered to the parish at this year's entertainment, and the duration of each item. Whether such an event is likely to occur next year is difficult to say at present. I was a trifle bitter, but I am now coming through to a place where I just want to hit someone.

Emily Townsend: Knitting to musical accompaniment - five minutes.

Georgina Weft and Gloria Pope:
Bereavement counselling jokes - five grave minutes.

Hilary Tuttsonson: Amusing anecdotes gleaned from several successful years running a first-class bed and breakfast establish ment which offers substantial reductions to church members and their friends or visitors - five minutes.

George Pain: Making his bare stomach look like an orang-outan's face when he sucks it in hard - eleven seconds (booed off).

Professor Varden: A brief account of the molecular interaction between unsynthesised electrical disfunction and the quasi-protonic elements of atomic fusion - five years.

Norman Bewes: Impression of the Foreign Secretary, Robin Cook, peeling a potato - seven seconds, but wanted to do it over and over again. Refused to leave the stage, got quite aggressive, and had to be coaxed off by his wife and a friend.

Cynthia Pope (age 6): Bawling her eyes out because she couldn't face playing Twinkle, twinkle,Little Star in public on her violin after all, even though she'd been looking forward to it for ages - twenty-five seconds, eight seconds, thirty-seven seconds and two seconds.

Yorick Experimental Contemporary Christian Dance Group:
DANCING WITH BLINDFOLDS - A NEW PIECE USING INNER PERCEPTION INSTEAD OF NORMAL SIGHT TO PROVIDE AWARENESS OF SPACE AND SOLID OBJECTS - billed to last ten minutes, but cut short when two members of the group had to be rushed to Casualty with suspected concussion.

Thomas Grimaldi: Mussolini being hung from a lamppost - two deeply disturbing minutes

14p

THE SKULL

The Parish Magazine of St Yorick's, Gently Down   NOVEMBER

IN DARK NOVEMBER'S THICKEST MIST
EVEN G. PAIN MIGHT GET KISSED

FAITH IN ACTION

'Go and draw toward Mount Tabor . . .'

JUDGES 4 v6 AV

VICAR : THE REVEREND RICHARD HARCOURT-SMEDLEY D.D. TEL : 569604
CURATE : THE REVEREND CURTIS WARMVOLE B.D. TEL : 563957
CHURCHWEIRDEN : MISTER C. VASEY B.A. TEL : 563749
VICAR'S SECRETLY : C. B. DUDE C.T.A.B. TEL : 569604
SKILL CONTRIBUTIONS TO HENRY PITCHER 3, FOXGLOVE ROAD: 563328

A Letter from the Vicar

Introduced this month by Christine Fitt

ST. YORICK'S COMMUNION SERVICE

I am, as many of you know, the vicar's secretary. Just before leaving for his autumn vacation the Reverend Harcourt-Smedley instructed me to pass to the editor of The Skull his plans for a new service book for the church, suggesting that these should constitute his magazine letter for this month. Unfortunately he did not specify the exact location of these plans, but eventually, after much searching, I found the following notes in a drawer beside his bed. They are clearly notes made for possible inclusion at various points in the service, and they are much thumbed, almost as if he had been reading and checking them over and over again before going to sleep. They seem to have been written some time ago, but I am sure that cannot be so, as I know the vicar has been working on this project very recently. I feel quite sure that these must be the plans he intended the parish to see before any final decisions are made, and I am also absolutely certain that he will welcome comments on his return.

AT THE COMMENCEMENT OF THE SERVICE

Hardly anyone shall arrive on time for the beginning of the service. It shall not seem to occur to any of them that it matters. Before the opening hymn the minister shall make a joke. None shall laugh.

AT THE HYMNS

The congregation shall sing with wildly varying degrees of skill and volume. Hilda Worthington shall finish each line a split second after the rest of the congregation. Her singing shall resemble the sound made by a chicken which has sat on a sharp, live wire. Whensoever Dave Billings shall fill in for the regular organist all shall wish that they were dead. Jonathan Basset shall laugh at the noise produced by Dave Billings and be smacked by his jealous parents. Whensoever Vaughn Claridge shall smuggle in his squeeze-box and attempt to play it, he shall be restrained and removed by sundry appointed members of the congregation.

AT THE CHILDREN'S TALK

The children shall not understand the point of an instructive little story. They shall be asked a damn-fool question. They shall fail to respond. An embarrassing silence shall ensue. Parents shall hiss at their children to try to get them to speak up. The same two who always do, might.

CHILDREN'S INVOLVEMENT IN THE SERVICE

The children shall perform a little play. It shall be invisible and inaudible to all but the front row of the congregation. The children involved shall not understand what they are saying or doing. They shall be steered blankly from one position to another by two adults bending at the waist. The congregation shall be puzzled but enchanted.

Continued overleaf . . . .

PRAYER FOR THE MONTH
By Eileen Grable

Lord, we bring up before thee Glenda Andrews, and we thank thee that last month she took the trouble to pray for thine servant now writing. We pray for her and her friends, that they may all regain those gifts of sight and hearing which, in their cases, have clearly become sadly impaired, and we particularly pray for Glenda, that she might lose just sufficient humility to begin taking a healthy interest in her own affairs, and be less committedly focussed on the innocent activities of others. We would remember at this time the last visit payed to Glenda's home by thine humble servant, and we ask that the debilitating condition which was preventing our sister from adequately cleaning her house may now be easing. May she be increasingly aware of the way in which evil is so often met with retribution both in the spiritual and the temporal spheres of life, and may she be particularly aware that when she next encounters thy servant a theological discussion of great depth and intensity is likely to ensue. Finally, may her tongue be completely healed and may it never enter into that sadly diseased state again. **Amen.**

LOCAL SAYING
Sent in by Cordless O'Leary

When limping voles begin to stutter,
There'll be droppings in the gutter.

Continued from previous page

AT THE PRAISE TIME

Most of the congregation shall clap half-heartedly during the praise time. Some shall bare their teeth. Philip Jaws, his wife, and all the little Jaws shall clap and bob about with enormous enthusiasm but be completely out of time with the music. Whensoever Maude Glass shall lead the praise time she shall make a vague buzzing noise by strumming her guitar with her thumb and sing in a key appropriate to some quite different solar-system. Hugh Danby shall ask himself why he keeps on coming when he could go down the road to The Exclusive Living Church of the Final Word of Revelation. The minister shall wish he would.

AT THE COLLECTION

At that point in the Offertory prayer where minister and congregation say "Of thine own have we freely given thee" many shall feel guilt because they have morosely parted with seventeen pence.

AT THE SERMON

At the announcement of the sermon some shall sigh resignedly. Old Mrs. Williams shall settle to sleep. At least one mother shall keep her crying baby in. Hilary Tuttsonson on the front row shall lean towards the minister and put that annoying look of encouragement on her face. The leader of the children's work shall allow all the children back in just before the sermon finishes to spite the minister, who she thinks should be more aware of the needs of others. The minister shall glare impotently at her and them and resolve to sort this out once and for all as soon as the service finishes. At the ending of the sermon Mrs. Williams shall awake with a loud animal noise. Jonathan Basset shall receive a second smack.

AT THE RESPONSES

The congregation shall respond in a mumbled, dull monotone. They shall sound as if they are reluctantly agreeing to be tortured in the very near future.

AT THE PRAYER OF HUMBLE ACCESS

Hilda Worthington shall secretly think she probably is worthy to gather up the crumbs under his table.

AT THE PEACE

The congregation shall shuffle miserably around wondering who to kiss, who to hug and who to ignore. George Pain shall embrace the two most attractive women in the church for a quite unnecessarily protracted length of time. Mrs. Purbrick shall go to the toilet until it's all over.

AT THE COMMUNION

At first all shall dither and none shall approach the communion rail, then all shall approach the communion rail at the same time. A muddle shall ensue. Some of the congregation shall return to pews they were not previously occupying. Conflicts shall result and be conducted in sibilant whispers in sundry parts of the church. Many of the communicants shall worry about taking communion because they are such bad people. The minister shall know exactly how they feel.

AT THE GIVING OF THE NOTICES

The minister shall deliver all the notices. None shall listen, except for sundry regular members of the congregation who shall correct the minister on matters of detail by calling out as he goes along. The minister shall fume.

AT THE FINAL HYMN

Sundry members of the congregation shall be visibly annoyed about the minister insisting that the final, long hymn should be sung even though the service is already way over normal time because of communion. They shall ask themselves why he is not able to be more flexible. The minister shall take a certain pleasure in drawing it out as long as he possibly can.

AT THE SAYING OF THE GRACE TOGETHER

Mrs. Purbrick shall go to the toilet once more. The rest of the congregation shall ladle soupy grins over their shoulders and over each other. Jonathan Basset shall mime being sick and be smacked for a third time.

AT COFFEE TIME

The congregation shall become human beings again and display the warmth that was conspicuously lacking during the service. The children shall over-consume biscuits. George Pain shall greet newcomers warmly in the hope of being invited to Sunday Lunch.

POETRY CORNER
SOMETHING THAT HAPPENED TO ME
By Colin Vasey

One night in the church I saw

A glowing baby on the floor

When I touched it with my hand

It turned into a flower stand

The flower stand was hard and cold

But quite a pleasant shape to hold

I took it slowly up the aisle

And when I tried to make it smile

Stars came flying through the walls

They fell in sparkling waterfalls

That made my baby shine like gold

Though sadly it was no less cold

The lectern eagle rose to see

What precious thing I held to me

On seeing my poor flower stand

It did not even try to land

But shattered through a

          stained-glass pane

Amid the shower of coloured rain

I left, but as I closed the door

A baby glowed upon the floor

HOUSEHOLD HINT

COLDS

Sent in by Alice Williams

Heavy colds are nasty, but here's a well-tried remedy that never failed when my mother used it on us as children. Remove all clothes, sit in a sink filled with crushed ice, place feet in a bowl of boiling water, chew a slice of lemon, and sniff tepid salt-water up your nose. There would sometimes be three of us kids sitting in a row in our big old kitchen sink! We made our own fun in those days.

WASH YOUR DIRTY LINEN WITH SIMON BLEACH

Q. Dear Mister Bleach,
I am seven and I do not beleeve in Father Christmas any more. It is them. They come in when you are asleep and put the presents there then they eat the minse pie and drink the sherry they put their there selves. I asked my mum but she will not tell me the truth. I asked my dad but he said ask your mum. It is obvius it is them and this Christmas I am going to stay awake and see them. All that elves stuff. And reindeer. It is them. There isn't a Father Christmas.
Cherry Andrews

A. Dear Cherry,
Thank you for your interesting letter. I consider it very right and proper that seven-year-olds like yourself should question things that have been told to them as fact by their parents over the years. Why should you be expected to swallow stories about reindeer and elves and silly stuff like that? In your letter you state quite clearly and definitely that you do not believe in Father Christmas. I respect that view, and so, I am quite sure, will Father Christmas himself. I shall be passing your letter directly on to him in the very near future, and I feel confident that he will react to it in the best and most appropriate way. It is very brave of you to prefer truth to a silly old bag full of mere presents.
Simon

● ● ● ● ● ● ● ● ● ● ● ● ● ● ●

Dear Readers,
Regular perusers of my column are invited to write to me, saying which single occurrence at St. Yorick's made them laugh most during the past year. Don't be too sensitive when it comes to naming names, will you? After all, if we can't laugh at ourselves, there's something very wrong. Right? So write. The best one gets published in the December Skull, and wins a fitting prize.
Simon

● ● ● ● ● ● ● ● ● ● ● ● ● ● ●

Q. Dear Simon Bleach,
I suppose you thought your response back in March to my letter about such creatures as herring hilariously funny. I did not. I care about all denizens of the deep, even if you don't. Wales, for example, have been given a place in which to play by God. Make a joke about that if you can.
Hilda

A. Dear Hilda,
I can assure you that I have no intention of making a joke about anything so sacred as Cardiff Arms Park.
Simon

● ● ● ● ● ● ● ● ● ● ●

SP🔦TLIGHT 6

THE CURATE
By Henry King

I set off with the usual reporting gear to do my last Spotlight interview of the year. This time I shall be speaking to the curate, Curtis, who lives in a small house belonging to the church in Apsley Gardens. I have never been here before. It is quite dark by the time I arrive, but there are lights blazing through every window in the house, and none of the curtains seem to be drawn. I get a sort of vague impression of people swirling around in every room doing all sorts of things.

As I am about to knock on the front door it swings open and two laughing young people more or less fall through the doorway, slam the door behind them, and disappear into the darkness without appearing to notice me. I knock again, and this time the door is opened by Curtis who has a telephone glued to one ear. The telephone's lead is at its furthest stretch from somewhere inside. He smiles and beckons enthusiastically for me to come through the porch into the hall, then, at the same time as he is speaking on the phone, he does a complicated mime with one hand in which he is twiddling something, then filling something, then pouring something, then tipping something into something else.

KNITTING

After knitting my brows and gesticulating questioningly back, I finally gather that he is inviting me to make myself a drink in the kitchen. I sqeeze past him in the hall and wander through to find the kitchen, which turns out to have four or five people of about my age crammed closely together round a small table with bibles and some wine and cheese and crusty bread. They look very happy and comfortable and I wish I was one of them, but feel very unsure about how one would go about being part of what they are doing. They are very welcoming. They ask who I am and invite me to have a glass of wine and some food, but I am shy and tell them that I have to interview the curate, so I'll just make myself some coffee and then leave them in peace. They tell me I'm welcome any Friday if I want to join them. I know I would really like to, but silently ask myself if I'll ever have the nerve. I reply to myself - maybe.

I find all the stuff to make my coffee, then carry it back to the hall, where Curtis is still talking on the phone. He smiles and nods encouragingly when he sees the coffee mug in my hand, then pretends to frown fiercely, jabbing a thumb into his chest, as if to say, "Where's mine, then?"

I leave my mug on the hall-stand and go back to the kitchen. There is a sort of warm glow in me about being there, not feeling like a guest, and knowing where things are this time. The people round the table remember my name. As I make the second mug of coffee I think to myself that they seem to do an awful lot of laughing and patting of each others' shoulders.

When I get back to the hall with Curtis's coffee he is still speaking on the phone. He grins and nods and gives me a thumbs-up on seeing his coffee, then indicates with his finger that I should go through a door on the opposite side of the hall. For some silly reason I assume that this room will be empty. It is not. There is a young teenage couple sitting on the sofa, very close together, holding hands. I have met them before. Their names are Dorothy James and Jacob Westbrook. I believe they are 'going out' They smile a little wanly at me.

FLOPS

Curtis comes in rubbing the palms of his hands together and says, "Right, where's that coffee?" He picks it up from the small table where I have placed it

carefully on a used envelope, takes a sip, then says, "Right, you two, time's up! Feel a bit clearer, do you?"

They nod their heads rather dolefully, but Dorothy gives Curtis a hug as they go out of the room, and I hear her thanking him for something out in the hall. There are a few moments more of murmured conversation, then the front door slams. Curtis comes back into the room and slumps down into the sofa where they were sitting. He sips his coffee again, then says, "Right, Henry, sorry to keep you waiting. Good to see you. Spotlight, isn't it? Fire away! I'm all ears - so they tell me. Ha-ha!"

I take out my notebook and pen and say, "Right, could I start by asking you if - "

The phone rings. Curtis leaps from his chair and disappears into the hall. I hear him explaining that he has a visitor. He comes back in, shuts the door, and flops down again. He says, "Sorry about that - right! Fire away!"

FLABBERGASTED

I say, "I'd like to ask you if - "

There is a tapping from the hall. One of the people who were sitting round the table in the kitchen puts his head round the door. He says, "Sorry, Henry. Sorry, Curtis, it's Phil - you know. Could you come?"

There is a pause while Curtis seems to debate inwardly, then he jumps to his feet and says, "Sorry, Henry - two seconds."

He returns in two or three minutes

and says, "I repent! Forgive me! Off you go. You'd like to ask me if..."

I say, "Look, this is obviously a vey busy time for you. Would it be better if I came back when you'd got more time? It's no problem to change the day, honestly."

Curtis says, "Oh, no, there won't be a better day than this. I chose my day off specially so that we wouldn't be interrupted too often."

I am flabbergasted. I say, "Your - ?"

The phone rings. Curtis springs from the sofa and disappears into the hall again. His head reappears round the door with the phone stuck to his ear again. He grimaces and shakes his head and rolls his eyes as though he is simply not going to be able to end the call quickly. I sigh and drink my coffee and wait. When I hear the phone going back on the hook I prepare myself, and as Curtis comes in I ambush him with my question before anything else can happen.

GRIND

I say very rapidly, "I'd like to ask you if you and the vicar manage to relate well to each other, bearing in mind that you seem to be very different in your individual approaches to ministry."

Curtis screws his face up as if he doesn't quite understand the question, then says, "The boss and I? Course we get on well. Richard's a great man - bit barky at times, but never known him actually bite very hard. The thing is, Henry, old chap, we are what we are, and

I'm lucky enough to have found myself in a parish with a vicar who doesn't mind me being me, as long as he doesn't have to be there to grind through some of the things that happen because of me being me. With me?"

I say, "My second question is about - "

The front door bell rings. Curtis lifts a finger and we wait in silence for a moment. There is the sound of someone opening the front door. Curtis smiles and settles back comfortably into his chair.

I say, "My second question is about - "

There is a knock at the sitting-room door. It opens. A very pretty girl in jeans and jumper, about the same age as the curate, opens the door and smiles charmingly at me before speaking to Curtis. I ask myself what you have to do to qualify for one of these wonderful women who are never with me.

The girl says, "Curtis, darling, there's a bit of an emergency. I can cope for a while, but it's you they want really. We'll be upstairs, okay? Sorry..."

Curtis invites me to carry on, but his eyes tell me that his heart is no longer in this interview, it is upstairs dealing with the emergency.

I leave shortly afterwards, promising myself that, if I can find the courage, I shall come back one Friday for that meeting in the kitchen.

I know the interview didn't really get going, but I'm glad Curtis is at St. Yorick's.

NOTICEBOARD

SERVICES

SUNDAY

8:00 a.m. Holy Communion, Batman!

9:30 a.m. Flimsy Service

11:00 a.m. Morning Prayer

6:30 p.m. Eventing Prayer

WEDNESDAY

10:30 a.m. Costly Harmonium

The Ladies Circle meeting will be held on Thursday November 20th at Mrs. Tyson's, 36, Butterwick Avenue, and will begin at 7: 30 p.m. This month will be a bring-and-show evening, where ladies are invited to bring along items that they have made, drawn, painted, written or cooked, but *not* photographed please. Mrs. Walsh will start us off by passing around a joint and telling us how to make it go just that little bit farther, and Mrs. Salmons will follow with some pieces of cardboard that she found in a box at home the other day, which, she says, are really interestingly shaped. Come on, girls! Can you match that?

On Friday November 11th at 6.45 the 2nd Gently Down Guide Company will be addressed in the church hall by Mr. William Slater, described in newspapers as 'the most dangerous man in Britain'. Mr. Slater has served three lengthy terms in high-security prisons for armed robbery with violence, and two for grievous bodily harm. Parents should ensure that their daughters dress sensibly as the heating is not functioning adequately at present, and that each girl brings money with her, as it seems likely that a collection will be taken at some point to aid Mr. Slater's ministry.

The final P.C.C. meeting for this year is at 7 : 30 on Thursday November 27th at the vicarage. There are important matters to be dismissed, so don't cuss it, whatever you do.

JESUS & ZAK

ZAK HEARD THE CROWD COMPLAIN AND I GUESS WITH JESUS STANDING RIGHT THERE MAYBE HE WAS REMINDED OF THE REST OF JESUS SAYING 'RENDER UNTO CEASER...' THE BIT WHERE HE SAYS 'AND TO GOD THE THINGS THAT ARE GODS.

'LOOK, SIR,' ZAK SAID, 'I WILL GIVE HALF MY PROPERTY TO THE POOR!'

THE CROWD WERE VERY HAPPY. THEY WERE GETTING TAX REBATES OF FOUR TIMES THE AMOUNT THEY HAD PAID!

THE JERICHO WALL PAPER

TAX REBATE FOUR ALL!

A LOCAL TAX COLLECTOR, ZAK, PICTURE LEFT, WITH TWO PEOPLE HE HAD CHEATED HANDS BACK FOURFOLD. THE CHANGE CAME ABOUT AFTER A MEETING WITH JESUS.

ZAK SAYS THAT SOMEHOW JESUS MADE HIM FEEL TALL ON THE INSIDE. NO-ONE HAD EVER DONE THAT BEFORE. HE ALSO SAID THAT JESUS HAD TOLD HIM HE WAS NOW SAVED. ZAK NOW FEELS THE BEST WAY FOR HIM TO INVEST IN THE FUTURE IS TO FOLLOW THE FINANCIAL AND OTHER ADVICE OF JESUS.

MOST PEOPLE HAVE FORGIVEN ZAK FOR BEING MEAN, AFTER ALL IF JESUS HAS HOW CAN THEY NOT. ZAK IS VERY CONTENT AND DOES HIS JOB FAIRLY AND SPENDS A LOT OF TIME WITH THE POOR. HE EVEN GIVES HIS LIMO DRIVERS THE DAY OFF SOMETIMES

THAT'S NOT ALL ZAK DID. HE PAID BACK ALL THE PEOPLE HE HAD CHEATED, AND HE PAID THEM FOUR TIMES AS MUCH AS HE HAD STOLEN.

AND BECAUSE OF THE WAY JESUS HAS MADE HIM FEEL HE HAS DECIDED NOT TO TAX TALL PEOPLE!

THE SKULL

The Parish Magazine of St Yorick's, Gently Down — **DECEMBER**

DECEMBER! WHILE WE ALL BUY PRESENTS
TURKEYS TRY TO LOOK LIKE PHEASANTS

FAITH IN ACTION

'They drew lots. . .'

ACTS 1 V26

VICAR : THE REVEREND RICHARD HARCOURT-SMEDLEY D.D. TEL : 569604
CURATE : THE REVEREND CURTIS WARMLOVE B.D. TEL : 563957
CHURCHWEIRDEN : C. VASEY B.A. TEL : 563749
VICAR'S SECRETARY : CRAZZA TEL : 569604
SKULL CONTRIBUTIONS TO HENRY PITCHER 3, FOXGLOVE ROAD : 563328

A Letter from the Vicar

Deeply Bothered,

In this season of joy and good will I have already received a number of extremely acid communications regarding certain items in the 'New Communion Service' published in last month's issue of this magazine, and I am all too well aware of the letter that appears on the Simon Bleach page in this issue of the magazine. Well, of course, that communion service was *not* the new communion service, as I am sure dead Mr. Pitcher realised when he playfully allowed it to be printed. I have communicated to Mr. Pitcher my feeling that he has been something of a naughty man over this, and he has agreed to print the real service early in the new year. I have also enjoyed a moderately intensive little employer-to-employee chat with Miss Fitt, who so enterprisingly but misguidedly discovered the wrong document whilst I was away from the parish, and I have expressed to her a deep and sincere wish that, in future months, she should cement the probability of her continued employment by being just a shade more

careful in her approach to these things.

All I can say to those people who were mentioned by name in last month's outpouring is that they should feel flattered - yes, flattered - by their inclusion in a piece that, as I am quite sure most intelligent parishoners guessed, was intended to be a fun contribution to some future entertainment within the family of the church. Naturally, those named in the piece were selected entirely because of their capacity for enjoying a joke regarding themselves, and they would have been most closely consulted before any public reading took place.

The suggestion, expressed with quite unnecessary coarseness and vitriol in one letter, that my wife and I are in the nightly habit of 'cackling over the antics of the punters' is patently absurd and quite untrue.

Let us resolve to extend the hand of forgiveness to each other at this very special time of year, and may I wish the whole of St. Yorick's a very merry Christmas and a happy and successful new year.

From the desk of your vicar

Retched Hardgrot-Smiley

P.S. *I should add that whilst I sincerely regret any embarrassment that may have been caused by the incident referred to above, I absolutely refuse to continue the pattern that has developed whereby Jonathan Basset, whose family resides in the same road as ourselves, comes to the back door of the vicarage every day and menacingly demands sweets in return for an assurance that he will not weep movingly in his bedroom at home.*

A Poem for Christmas
TALKING TURKEY
By Sarah Forrest

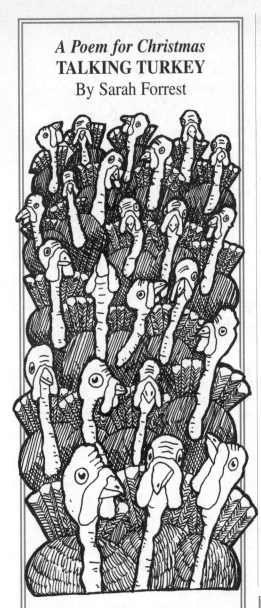

Gobble, gobble, turkey birds,
Gobble from the heart,
Gobble, gobble all you can,
Before the humans start.

Dear Sir,

May I place on record my deep and ongoing appreciation of the vicar's monthly litter. I sift carefully through it whenever it appears and invariably find something that I can really use in my life. May he continue to produce it for many a month to come.

Colin Vasey (willing churchwarden)

• • • • • • • • • • • • • • • • • • • •

Dear Mr. Pitcher,

Way back in September you said that you would give a small prize to anyone who solved the message that Helga Durr sent to the church. I think I have done it. What she meant to say was: Godspeed, and may we meet once more in the fullness of time. Is that it?

Janice, aged thirteen.

• • • • • • • • • • • • • • • • • • • •

Dear Janice,

Well done, you're absolutely right! And you'll be thrilled to hear that your prize is a ready-made, road-flattened, born-again toad made by the expert, Liz Turton (see Children's Corner this month), which you can either give to your dad, or keep for yourself. Happy inflating!

Henry Pitcher

LOCAL SAYING
Sent in by Ivy Tyson

An ankle sprained on Christmas night,
Brings apples from the Isle of Wight.

"MY DARLING HAMSTER..."

Nicol Corkrot. Published by Echo Books.
Reviewed by Simon Bleach

Nicol Corkrot is known primarily as a Christian speaker, but he has, of course, already had enormous success with his three preceding titles: My Darling Gerbil, My Darling Budgie and My Darling Goldfish. In the first of these bestselling books, we learn how God spoke with amazing clarity through Corkrot's gerbil, enabling the writer to interpret spiritual patterns made by his pet each morning in the bedding scattered at the bottom of its cage. Certain that these messages were intended for the whole church, Corkrot collected them into one volume which was, of course, published as 'My Darling Gerbil...' In his introduction to this book the author makes the following comment:

Naturally, there is no question of these messages adding to or taking away from scripture. If, however, you ask me whether the words received by my hamster actually are from God, well, naturally it's not for me to say, but, I mean - come on...

The sudden death from starvation of Corkrot's gerbil soon after publication, suggested that these messages would now cease, and they might well have done had it not been for Corkrot's publishers, who, drifting with the providential flow, presented him with the gift of a caged bird, arriving by carrier together with his latest royalty cheque. God graciously agreed to continue his communications through this budgie, and the second collection of messages was published with equal success in the following year.

'My Darling Goldfish...' is a similar volume, based on Corkrot's Spirit-led inter-pretation of the undulating movements of a silver carp, this creature being a successor to the budgie, whose final, and, presumably, rather too solidly secular communication regarding the need for a few scraps of food, somehow escaped Corkrot's notice.

The very successful team of God, Corkrot, Corkrot's publisher and Corkrot's latest pet continues with 'My Darling Hamster...', (the fish became rather err scaled down) which will no doubt sell as well as its companion volumes. Here is a fairly typi-cal extract from one of the daily messages:

'My Darling Hamster...

Tell your master that I totally agree with absolutely all the things he says about me and the church and life and being a proper Christian and everything. Tell him that if any nasty people start disagreeing with him, he is to ignore them and assume that they cannot possibly know what they are talking about. Tell him how much I appreciate the way in which he uses language in the media that can only be understood by people who are involved in a very small sector of the church, and encourage him to go on staring at people during meetings in that special way of his that makes them feel guilty even though they haven't done anything. Tell him my only small criticism is that his talks are just a tad too short. Four more points and another three-quarters of an hour should do the trick.

Now, regarding my instruction that everyone without exception who claims to be a Christian should be hearing from me daily through a pet animal of some kind...

Presumably these books will go on appearing until Corkrot runs out of pets or someone forgets to feed Corkrot. Either way, I shan't be reading them.

SAVED FROM THE EVIL FLAMING PITS OF AN EARTHLY HELL
By Billy 'The Blade' Scuzball.

Pulished by Kingdom Teddy Bear.   *Reviewed by Hilda Worthington*

This very spiritually based book begins with an absorbing chapter entitled 'I Grow up in a Filthy Vice-ridden Den of Oozing Corruption', in which we learn of Billy's early diet of rat entrails, and the way in which, every day, men laid bets on the time it would take him to fall from the tops of high buildings into the sewage-strewn alleys through which he crawled during the tear-soaked years of his lonely childhood.

Chapter Two also grips the attention immediately, and is called 'I learn to use a Knife on the Pimps, Perverts and Murderers who exist like Pigs in the Suppurating Dung of their own Vile Deeds.' For those who know nothing of the way in which such people live, this is a vividly dramatic introduction to the world that Billy Scuzball grew up in.

Chapter Three, 'I do some quite unbelievably Grotesque and Horrible things because no-one ever taught me they were wrong', and Chapter Four, 'All the Sordid Details of my Depraved Sex-life including things that you never thought Physically Possible' are equally enthralling, as are the following seven chapters, in which Billy continues to graphically describe the mire of sinful indulgence in which he wallowed for most of his life.

For me, the book tailed off a little in the postscript, where Billy talks about his conversion to Christianity, but overall it's a jolly good read, and what a relief to be able to give a constructive, spiritual book like this to your younger teenage children, who live in a society where inappropriate videos and books are, unfortunately, so easily available to them. A good stocking-filler!

OLD STANLEY SELF-MADE PROVES ME RIGHT By Sam Alien
Published by Churn Books.   *Reviewed by Dave Billings*

This book is written by Sam Alien, well known in church circles for his deeply held conviction that elderly members of churches should not just be allowed and encouraged, but *made* to go out and take part in children's activities during Sunday services. Most people are aware of Sam's background. He grew up with very little formal education, speaks with a strong regional accent, constantly leads meetings for elderly people by simply bashing the keys of a piano more or less at random, and believes that theology is pointless because it just confuses people and is snobby.

The main character in Sam's new book, Old Stanley, is an elderly man who sets out on a journey from Elderly-People-Not-Allowed-In-With-The-Children Land, in search of the legendary Elderly-People-Are-Allowed-In-With-The-Children Land. During his travels he meets Mister Highly-Educated-But-Completely-Useless who deliberately and maliciously sends him the wrong way, so that he finds himself sinking into the Swamp-of-Correct-Speech, from which he is rescued just in time by Good-John-Speak-as-you-like. Further adventures include encounters with the Boringly-Correct-Musical-Folk, who never get anything done because they are too busy trying to learn how to play their instruments perfectly, and a battle to cross the Desert of Snobby Theology without dying of thirst. Finally Stanley arrives at Elderly-People-Are-Allowed-In-With-The-Children Land, and all is well.

Perceptive readers might spot Sam Alien's own views peeping through here and there. All in all, a very subtle and meaningful allegory that can be read on a number of levels - well, one.

BOOK REVIEWS

A LOVELY PRESENT FOR THE DADDY WHO'S GOT EVERYTHING

BORN-AGAIN TOADS

Contributed by Liz Turton

Don't throw away those old used drinks cartons this Christmas, children, or the straws that come with them. After only a very little easy cutting and sticking, you can enjoy making an extra present to give Daddy - his very own, road-flattened, inflatable, born-again toad!

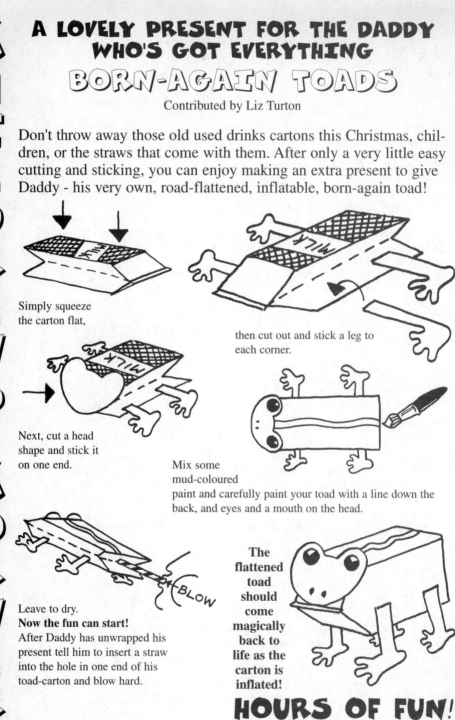

Simply squeeze the carton flat,

then cut out and stick a leg to each corner.

Next, cut a head shape and stick it on one end.

Mix some mud-coloured paint and carefully paint your toad with a line down the back, and eyes and a mouth on the head.

BLOW

Leave to dry.
Now the fun can start!
After Daddy has unwrapped his present tell him to insert a straw into the hole in one end of his toad-carton and blow hard.

The flattened toad should come magically back to life as the carton is inflated!

HOURS OF FUN!

WASH YOUR DIRTY LINEN WITH SIMON BLEACH

Q. Dear Simon,

Am I the only person in the parish who feels faintly puzzled by the fact that the church girl-guide troop appears to have been addressed at one of their meetings last month by a highly dangerous criminal? Are we not to hear the end of the story? Did Mr. William Slater turn nasty? Did he conduct an offering in his own inimitably felonious way? Did he grievously harm anyone's body? Were members of the troop so inspired by his powerful example that each is now striving towards the ultimate aim of being awarded the title 'Most Dangerous Girl-Guide in Britain'? Did the girls dress warmly enough?

Please forgive me if you think I sound a little negative. I will immediately make amends by offering constructive suggestions. Here is one. How about deciding that January will be 'Serial Killer Month' for all the St.Yorick guides? I feel sure that we could arrange for a crazed multiple murderer to be brought from some high security prison, handcuffed to several policemen, to talk to the girls about what sort of training and how many G.C.S.E's are required to get started on a career in homicidal mania.

Perhaps each of the girls could do a special project on the Nazi war criminal of their choice. Little miniature gallows could be fashioned from twigs, and Adolf Eichmann's face could be picked out in cotton on the sleeve of a uniform. That sort of project would be attractive, fun and really quite easy to do.

James

A. Dear James,

I decided not to publish the additional four pages of heavy sarcasm that had obviously given you so much pleasure to write. I think it just possible that you were perfectly aware of William Slater's very genuine and well documented conversion to the Christian faith, a faith which, you may recall, offers complete forgiveness to those who repent, whether they are violent criminals or caustic, embittered bigots.

Simon

• • • • • • • • • • • •

Q. Dear Simon Bleach,

We, the undersigned, are shocked, hurt and extremely angry about the way in which we were ridiculed in the ludicrous and quite unfunny parody of a communion service that appeared in last month's magazine. Mrs. Purbrick in particular is quite distraught, and wishes to state publicly that she *never* goes to the toilet, whilst Philip Jaws has asked us to point out that he and his family bob in the Spirit, and should not therefore be criticised. We condemn the vicar for being insensitive enough to write it, we condemn Christine Fitt for being foolish enough to pass it on, and we condemn Henry Pitcher for indulging his warped sense of humour by publishing it. How this sort of behaviour can be equated with any claim on the part of these people to hold Christian principles is a complete mystery to us. We are now seriously considering our position with regard to continued membership of the church. Do you not agree that what has happened is disgraceful?

Yours Faithfully:
Hilda Worthington
Dave Billings

The Jaws family
Maude Glass
Hugh Danby
Mrs. Williams
H. Tuttsonson
Mrs. Purbrick
Mrs. Williams again
Glenda Andrews

P.S. Non-signatories :
Vaughn Claridge - not allowed to sign because we agree with the vicar.
Jonathan Basset - suspiciously unmoved.
George Pain - because he 'liked being in it'.

P.P.S. It is true that **Glenda Andrews** was not actually mentioned in the offending piece, but she tells us that she has always felt that the vicar has a down on her, and that it's typical of him to leave her out.

A. Dear shocked, hurt and extremely angry people,
It may be a disgrace, but I feel quite sure that, like me, the rest of the parish awaits with breathless expectancy the outcome of this remarkable opportunity for you to demonstrate that you are more Christian than the vicar, the vicar's secretary, or the editor of this magazine. When you say that you condemn these four people, presumably you mean, in some obscure sense, that you forgive them, do you? Or perhaps you are suggesting that when Jesus commanded us to forgive our brothers and sisters unto seventy times seven, he winked heavily and added in a whisper, "Of course, that doesn't apply to Richard Harcourt-Smedley, Christine Fitt or Henry Pitcher."
As for the idea of discontinuing your membership of the church, well, yes! What a wonderful witness. Punishing the rest of the church community for what someone else has done is another aspect of Christian living that has been much underused in the last two-thousand years. Go for it!
Simon

• • • • • • • • • • • • • •

Q. Dear Simon,
Please pass on my congratulations to the editor on the spoof communion service in last month's mag. What a scream - and what a nerve, naming people by name like that. Spiced things up no end. You're right - she does sing like a chicken sitting on something sharp. Well done!
Scott

A. Dear Scott,
I have passed your congratulatory letter on to the editor. He's framing it.
Simon

• • • • • • • • • • • • • •

Q. Dear Mister Bleach,
Is it too late to not send my letter to Father Christmas? Please don't send it. It is not them. It is him. Don't send it. Please don't send it. Please Mister Bleach. I am begging you DON'T SEND IT.
Cherry Andrews

P.S. Don't send it.

A. Dear Cherry,
You are a very lucky girl. I thought I had sent your letter off, but when I was looking through my drawer the other day, there it was, tucked into one of my old bibles. It would make a good page marker. I am sending it back to you, and I wanted to say that, when I think about it, I am sure you have made the right decision.
Simon

• • • • • • • • • • • • • •

Q. Dear Simon Not-from-Durham-writes-rubbish-about-miracles Bleach,
The funniest thing by far that happened this year was when you came up the front to read the lesson a couple of months ago, no doubt thinking in your usual clever-dick way that you didn't have to prepare the passage because your sight-reading is so superior to eveyone else's. Then, when you got to the lectern, you found that the

bit of scripture you had to read was full of long, almost unpronounceable Jewish names, didn't you? What followed was better than a night at the cinema, and - guess what? I got hold of the tape recording they make of the service for bedridden folk, and I've copied out your bit, as near as I can get it, and I enclose it for publication in The Skull, if you dare:

SIMON : (SETTING OFF IN HIS USUAL ARRO-GANTLY CONFIDENT TONES) And the king saith unto him, "I know thy name well (HORROR - STRUCK PAUSE) Abim - in - im - ad - im - in - ai. Abidinim - Adiminim - Ambididni - Abiniminadiminai. (CLEARS THROAT) And I also know thy father, Hamil - in - im - il - ib - lim. Hamilinimiliblimil - Aliminium (GROANS) Hamilinimiliblim - blim. I knew him in the city that is called (AGONISED GROAN) Eg - shaz - lwer - gnan - dai - ga. Egshazlwergnandaiga - Egshazlwergnandaiga - Egshazlwergnandaiga, and also (WITH PATHETIC RELIEF) at Gad."

"Thou speakest well, oh, king," saith ABINIMI - NIDIMINI - DIMI -

MIDIMIDIMUM, "that thou knowest my father, HAMINLIMINILIBLIMINIL at EGLW - EGLW - EGLW - EGLW - EGLW - EGLW - EGLW - at GAD."

This is the word of the Lord - sort of...

Wouldn't have missed it for the world. Prize please.
Victor Clements

A. Dear Victor,
You are fortunate that I am a tolerant, broadminded, laid-back sort of guy who doesn't mind everyone in the parish having a laugh at his expense. You are even more fortunate that I have a wife who threatened to leave me if I refused to publish your letter and award you the prize. So, the good news is that you do get the prize, and the even better news, I'm sure you'll agree, is that the prize is a copy of my slim volume 'Public Speaking in Church'. Rushing it to you now, as they say in the ads. Hope you are not too busy planning next year's follow-up to your blazing Pentecost success, and therefore have lots of time to enjoy it.
Simon

• • • • • • • • • • • • • •

Q. Dear Simon,
I don't know if you can help with this query, but several of us have been wondering about the ini-

tials that appear after the name of the vicar's secre-tary on the front page of The Skull each month. The vicar is a D.D., presumably Doctor of Divinity, and B.D. and B.A. are equally famil-iar, but what is indicated by the initials C.T.A.B.? It is not a qualification that any of us have ever heard of. We have presumed that it is a diploma awarded after an advanced secretarial course of some kind. Perhaps you could find out for us.
Several Of Us

A. Dear Several Of You,
I have indeed asked Miss Fitt, or Crazza, as she now wishes to be known, about the initials you mention, and she was more than happy to supply the information because, she says, she is in love, and doesn't care about anyone knowing anything at all about her. I counselled her to keep the following fact to herself, but she insisted that it should be published, so here it is. When she first came to work for the vicar, Crazza was a little embarrasssed about having no letters to put after her name like the others who are mentioned on the front page each month, so she invented some. C.T.A.B stands for CAN TYPE A BIT.
Simon

• • • • • • • • • • • • • •

A CHRISTMAS HOUSEHOLD HINT

EMPTIES

Sent in by Maude Dent

At Christmas-time empty milk bottles seem to breed, don't they? Well, how about this for an idea? On Christmas Day, perhaps at a point when things seem to have temporarily gone a little flat, go quietly into the kitchen without telling anyone and collect together ten empty milk bottles. Stand them on the kitchen table and put each of your ten fingers and thumbs into a seperate bottle. You will find it quite easy to keep the bottles in place after you lift your hands. Now, burst into the room in which most people are gathered, and, clinking the bottles together with your fingers and thumbs, shout out loudly, "Edward Bottlehands!". Things won't be flat after that! Why not let the kids have a go when you've finished?

How beautiful on the mountains are the feet of those who bring good news? The answer is - not very, if they haven't had those ugly corns treated. Christian chiropodist. Special Yuletide reductions for those who want to make use of me the living leg end. **Ring 560278**

There will be a midnight service this year, but after our problems last time it has been decided that any incidents of drunkeness will be dealt with most severely. The opening carol will be 'God Help you Merry Gentlemen.'

Our Christmas Day service will be a Family Service, and will begin at 10 : 30 a.m. The vicar's wife will encourage children to come to the front and display the contents of their stockings to the congregation, just as she has been doing every year since she first came to the parish.

A **'Nearly-There New Year's Eve Party'** will be held at the Jaw home, 25, Forwill Drive, from 8 : 00 p.m. until midnight. Admission by unsaved friend and any bottle or carton of soft-drink. Choruses will be sung.

NOTICEBOARD

₯₥₳₰₰ ₱₥₳₰₳₦₳₥₰

₱₰₥₰₳₳₥

8:00 a.m. ₩ollp Communism (gnus)

9:30 a.m. ₱laming ₱ervice

11:00 a.m. ₥ovinȝ ₱raper

6:30 p.m. ₢veninȝ ₱raper

₩₢₰₥₢₱₰₳₥

10:30 a.m. ₩olp Composition

At 5: 30 p.m. on Wednesday 24th December (Christmas Eve) we shall be holding our Christingle service, in the course of which children are given an orange and a candle in symbolic welcome of the baby Jesus, the light of the world, into our midst. Members of the Mother and Toddler group that meets regularly in the church hall are specially invited to attend this very moving service, but please keep very small children at the back, and note that the church and its servants and employees can not be held responsible for damage or injury caused in any way whatsoever by the flame of the said candles, or by any object or surface that that has been heated or ignited by that flame.

A warm welcome to all!

The parish Carol Service will be held on Sunday December 21st at 6 : 30 p.m. in the church. A chance to relax for those who are itching to get away from the Christmas rash.

The parish carol-singing expedition will set forth on Friday 19th of December at 6 : 30p.m. And let's have a few younger folk this year! Please gather outside the vicarage for the distribution of snogsheets. If you play an instrument bring it along. Vaughn Claridge will be in New Malden.

This month's Ladies Circle meeting will be held on Thursday December 18th at 36, Butterwick Avenue. This will be a 'Singalong-a-Satan' evening (he may even put in an appearance!), with mince-pies, sherry and, just before our husbands take us home, the exchanging of small gits.

Single Anglican lady wishing to remain anonymous in case of embarrassing her employer at the vicarage, would like to respond to George Pain's very moving lines in the November magazine by saying that she has been chewing moss, and it works! She would be very happy to kiss him in any month of the year, and that includes the mistless ones in which he is clearly risible.

A VERY
MERRY
CHRISTMAS
TO
ALL OUR
READERS!!!

If you thought this year's
magazines were good, wait
till you see next year's!
You ain't seen nuthin' yet!
Henry Pitcher

Also by Adrian Plass and available
from HarperCollins*Publishers*...

Father to the Man
and other stories

What is a forty-something bloke to do when he and his wife don't seem to talk any more, his teenage son is alienated from him and his best mate – reliable drinking companion for many years – suddenly and inexplicably becomes a Christian?

What do a family do when a much-loved grandparent dies unexpectedly and a freshly baked cake is discovered, obviously intended to be eaten when all were together?

These are just two of the dilemmas to be addressed among many others in this latest collection of stories from the writer who created the Sacred Diarist and *An Alien at St Wilfred's*.

The Sacred Diary of
Adrian Plass aged 45³/₄

Illustrated by Dan Donovan

Certainly a little older, perhaps just a tiny bit wiser, Adrian Plass was amazed when his account of 'serious spiritual experiences' in *The Sacred Diary of Adrian Plass aged 37¾* became widely read and appreciated as a funny book! More books have followed and now he's in demand as a public speaker all over the place. As we follow him to a variety of venues the reason why Christian speakers need travelling mercies becomes abundantly clear!

Many of the characters we met in the first *Sacred Diary* are with us again – Leonard Thynn, the Flushpools, Gerald (grown up now, of course!), Adrian's wife Anne, voluptuous Gloria Marsh, Edwin (the wise church elder) and the ever-religious Richard and Doreen Cook – as well as one or two new characters; Stephanie Widgeon, for instance, who only seems to have one thing to say…

One last question – what is a banner ripping seminar?

Stress Family Robinson

The Robinson family – mother, father, two teenage sons and a six-year-old daughter who is everybody's favourite – are a typical Christian family – or are they?

Does life behind the front door of the tall, thin Victorian semi-detached where they live match up to (or even resemble) the image they convey at their parish church?

The one person who knows the Robinsons almost better than they know themselves is dear Dip Reynolds – trusted friend-extraordinaire who has a few surprising secrets of her own to reveal…

Adrian Plass Classics

The Growing Up Pains of Adrian Plass

View from a Bouncy Castle

Cabbages for the King

Adrian Plass's unique perspective on life and faith can be enjoyed once more in this omnibus edition of three of his best-selling books. In *The Growing Up Pains of Adrian Plass*, we meet the real Adrian Plass, as opposed to his fictional counterpart in the *Sacred Diary* series. *Cabbages for the King* and *View from a Bouncy Castle* are collections of stories, sketches and poems which celebrate both the profundity and the absurdity of life, while making keen points about the gospel. Underlying Adrian's irrepressible humour is his passionate conviction that God embraces us in our weakness and vulnerability, and that we need to gain a child-like perspective in order to understand just how much he loves us.

An Alien at St Wilfred's

- Who wants to poison the organist?

- Why is the overhead projector so very annoyed?

- Who made the vicar burst into tears in his own pulpit?

- What on earth is happening to the church lighting?

- Why did four sane Anglicans meet on top of the tower in a raging storm?

- What is going on?

It's very simple – there's an alien at St Wilfred's!

This is the story of Nunc, the small alien, who comes to Earth and learns to speak Prayer Book English – all told in the inimitable style of best-selling author Adrian Plass.